Book Level __

AR Points ___

RANGER'S APPRENTICE

THE ROYAL RANGER BOOK 6

ARAZAN'S WOLVES

RANGER'S APPRENTICE

THE ROYAL RANGER BOOK 6

ARAZAN'S WOLVES

JOHN FLANAGAN

VIKING

VIKING

An imprint of Penguin Random House LLC, New York

First published in Australia by Penguin Random House Australia, 2023
First published in the United States of America by Viking,
an imprint of Penguin Random House LLC, 2023

Visit us online at PenguinRandomHouse.com.

Library of Congress Cataloging-in-Publication Data is available.

ISBN 9780593463840

1   3   5   7   9   10   8   6   4   2

Printed in the United States of America

BVG

Text set in Adobe Jenson Pro

RANGER'S APPRENTICE

THE ROYAL RANGER BOOK 6

ARAZAN'S WOLVES

1

THE THREE BROTHERS HAD BEEN HARD AT WORK SINCE THE
sun had shown the first traces of pink over the hills to the east.
Now it was slowly sinking to the rim of the western cliffs, and
Owen ap-Jones, the eldest of the three, straightened his back
painfully and leaned on the handle of his hoe.

"That's enough for today," he said.

Wearily, he surveyed the field he and his brothers had been
working on all day. It was poor ground, hard and filled with
rocks, and difficult to till. The task wasn't made any easier by
the quality of the tools they had to use. The metal was soft and
easily deformed. Owen glanced down at the blade of his hoe
and frowned as he noticed three new notches in the edge and
one section where the blade had curled back on itself. He'd
have to hammer that out overnight and file out the notches before the tool would be serviceable again. Even though the field
wasn't a big one, he estimated that it would take them another
two days' hard labor hacking rows, removing rocks and turning
the thin topsoil before they could begin to plant their crop of
beans.

He shrugged. Life as a farmer in Celtica was hard. The land

was better suited to mining. But there were no deposits of iron or silver on their land, and their only choice was to farm or starve.

Gryff and Dai, Owen's younger brothers, both stopped working as he spoke.

"Curse this ground," Gryff said bitterly. He kicked at a rock close by his foot, sending it skittering. "We'll spend hours, days, hacking away at it, and for what?"

Neither of the others answered, so he continued. "For beans. Beans! Who can live on beans?"

Dai shrugged. "Well, we do," he replied.

Gryff was the youngest brother and was inclined to be the moodiest of the three. Owen and Dai had learned to accept life as it came. Complaining about their lot, they knew, was a waste of time and energy. Life was what it was, and no amount of whining or ranting would change that. Their father had died at a relatively young age, worn out from the effort of tending their field and providing for his family. At least, Owen thought, the three brothers could share the work.

"Let's go," he said now, putting an arm around his young brother's shoulders. "Mam will have supper ready for us."

"Bean soup," Gryff muttered angrily. Although, at the thought of food, his stomach rumbled. They had eaten at midday, stopping for half an hour for a meal of bread and cheese washed down with watered ale. There had been no breakfast. The farm could only provide two meals a day, both of them simple and without any appetite appeal.

"Bean soup, bread and cheese," he continued, listing the unvarying contents of their daily menu. "Who can live on that? The miners eat meat twice a week, and they have porridge on the other days."

"So they say," Owen replied. He wasn't sure that the miners in their village of Poddranyth were completely trustworthy about the quality of the meals they enjoyed. Miners were notoriously mendacious. Still, he thought, they probably lived better than he and his brothers did.

"We should be ready to plant in another two days," he said, hoping to change the subject.

"Two days!" Gryff exclaimed. "Two days grubbing and hacking and hoeing. If we had a donkey and a plow we'd get it done in half the time!"

"We don't have either," Owen said in a reasonable tone.

But Gryff wasn't to be diverted from his litany of complaints. "David ap-Davis has both. He could lend them to us!"

David ap-Davis was another farmer in Poddranyth. But he had three fields, all on better, more fertile ground than the single rocky plot that the ap-Jones brothers worked. As a result, his crops were larger and he could afford to sell some of his extra produce to the miners in the village.

"He'd charge us for them," Dai put in gloomily.

Gryff's anger flared once again. "Aye, that he would! And at a crippling price! He'd never think of lending them to help us."

"Why should he?" Owen said. "A mule only has so many hours of work in its life. And chances are our rocky ground would damage the plow. He'd have every right to charge us."

There was no real answer to that, Gryff knew. But his brothers' stolid acceptance of the life they shared continued to annoy him. He glared at the rocky ground as they trudged away from the half-prepared field toward the village. It was a two-kilometer walk, and mostly uphill. Their elongated shadows preceded them, rippling strangely over the uneven ground.

Owen sighed, glad that Gryff's complaining had finally died away. It was the same every day. His brother would continue to complain about their lot until he came to realize that complaining would never change it. It was their fate to labor in the rocky earth, hacking and ripping at it with their inefficient tools, planting a new crop each season and subsisting on what they could grow. They had the field and three goats, who provided them with enough milk for their cheese and a little extra to trade for flour. In addition, their mother kept half a dozen hens who gave them a meager supply of eggs and, on rare occasions, a bird to roast or boil.

And that was life for a farmer in Poddranyth: an unvarying, repetitive pattern of exhausting work, constant, nagging hunger, boredom and weariness.

There was little joy in it. But it was what it was. And Owen knew there were others who were in even harder straits than the ap-Joneses. Eventually, he thought, Gryff would come to realize it and accept it.

They crested a hill on the path. On one side of the narrow road, the ground fell away in a steep, shale-covered slope into a valley. On the other, the cliffs rose sheer and bleak. In the distance, a kilometer away, they could see the gray huddle of houses that made up Poddranyth. There were a score of them—all similarly built from stone and weathered timber, with dried mud sealing the gaps between the uneven surfaces. The shallow-pitched roofs were covered in split-stone shingles, and smoke rose from most of the stumpy chimneys.

"Nearly home," said Owen, with a note of relief in his voice. At least the house would be warm, and that would be a welcome sensation. The perspiration of the day had soaked his clothes, and it was cold under the evening wind. If Ma's chickens had provided a few extra eggs today, they might be able to trade for a jar of ale from the small tavern that served the village. It didn't often happen—the hens were as poorly fed as the family—but he could hope. Maybe he could—

The thought of home comforts was interrupted by a low-pitched, blood-curdling growl. The hair on the back of Owen's neck stood on end in a primitive reaction to the sound. He stopped in his tracks and looked around, noting that his brothers had also come to a halt.

"What was—" Gryff began, but Dai nudged him with his elbow to silence him.

Instinctively, the three brothers edged closer together, gripping their hoes protectively, raising them not as tools but as primitive weapons. They stood back to back, facing outward as they searched their surroundings for the source of the threatening sound.

It came again, louder this time and with a definite note of challenge in it, as if reacting to the sight of the men's hoes. And again, the brothers' blood ran cold at the sound.

"Look," said Owen, gesturing at the cliff above and behind them.

Five meters up, a narrow ledge ran along the glistening rock face. On it was crouched a nightmare shape.

It was at least three meters long and stood a meter and a half high at its front shoulders. Its front legs were longer than the rear, giving it a hunchbacked appearance. It had the face and general appearance of a wolf, but no wolf they had ever seen or heard of was the size of this one. Its powerful shoulders were tensed, and the thick ruff of fur around its throat was raised, making it appear even larger than it was.

It was covered in thick, matted fur, mainly gray but marked with several black patches. A black stripe ran from its left shoulder down the leg.

As they watched, stricken with terror, it opened its massive jaws, baring long, yellow canines, and snarled again, louder this time and even more threatening. Its yellow eyes looked around for a path down to the roadway where the brothers stood transfixed.

"Move . . . slowly," Owen said in a soft voice, and huddled together in a defensive circle, the three men began to edge away from the horrific creature. As they moved, it raised its head and roared out a challenge to them.

"Stop!" Dai said, and they froze in place. The creature lowered its head, and the shattering snarl died away to a low, threatening rumble. Again, it scanned the cliff face between it and them, searching for a way down to the roadway.

It took a pace down, finding a footing in the rock. Then another.

The three farmers moved again, shuffling away from it. As they moved, its head came up and the massive fangs were bared once more. The warning snarl froze them in their tracks. As they stopped, it stepped down a further two paces, its heavily clawed paws seeking and finding purchase in the steep rock face of the cliff where none seemed possible.

"What is it?" whispered Gryff, his throat dry with terror.

"It's a direwolf," Owen told him, in the same low tones. A direwolf: a beast out of myth and fable, belonging to an earlier age. As a lad, Owen had heard tales whispered around the fire about these huge, savage killers. But as he grew older, he began to believe the stories of direwolves were just that—stories, fables, myths. Direwolves didn't exist. Or, if they ever had, they had disappeared from the earth centuries ago.

Yet here was one facing them. Stalking them.

His knees shook underneath him as the killer came farther down the cliff face. Then, with one final bound, it covered the last two meters and landed, crouching, on the path behind them. A cold hand of terror clutched Owen's heart. The beast took another pace toward them. It was barely ten meters away now. Its eyes locked on them, gleaming with hatred. Its massive lips curled back from its yellow fangs, and drool dripped from the fangs onto the dirt of the road. Head down, heavy tail sweeping ominously from side to side, the creature began to advance on them.

Owen felt his bladder trying to release with terror and fought against the sensation. Somehow, he knew, if he showed his abject terror, that would be the end of him. The battered hoe in his hands seemed a totally ineffective defense, but he brandished it anyway, interposing it between him and the dreadful beast that was slowly slinking closer and closer. Any moment now, he sensed, it would—

"Run!" screamed Gryff, his nerve finally breaking. And as he said the word, he turned and bolted down the track toward Poddranyth. A split second later, Dai followed him, running as if the hounds of hell were on his heels—as indeed one was.

Owen faced the beast alone for a second. Enraged by the movement of the two men, it raised its head and howled in fury. As it did so, Owen turned and fled after his brothers.

But he was older than they were, and his joints were stiff. His muscles were sore and weary after a day of hard labor in the fields. He heard the quick rush of the dread creature behind him as it bounded in pursuit, heard its feet growing closer, claws scraping and rasping on the stones underfoot, and he realized he would never outrun it.

Ahead of him, Dai and Gryff heard a long, drawn-out scream from their older brother as the direwolf ran him down, dragging him to the ground.

Then the screaming stopped.

2

WILL HEAVED ON THE CORD ATTACHED TO THE HANGING HAY bale and set it swinging back and forth like a pendulum.

"Turn!" he shouted.

Twenty-five meters away, Maddie pivoted so that her back was to the swinging bundle. She held her bow in her left hand, an arrow nocked and pointing downward.

Will waited another few seconds, then called again. "Turn!"

Maddie turned again, the bow coming up and the arrow moving back to full draw. She locked her gaze on the small hay bale, measuring its movement and speed for a few seconds, then released.

The arrow sped across the intervening distance and thudded into the tightly packed hay, just to the left of the red circle painted in its center. She grinned at her mentor. Will raised one eyebrow.

"Pretty good, eh?" she said. The bale was festooned with half a dozen arrows, all set toward the center.

Will shrugged. "You missed."

She regarded him indignantly, her hands on her hips. He was a hard taskmaster. "I've hit the bale half a dozen times!" she protested.

"And you've missed the red circle half a dozen times," he pointed out.

Maddie rolled her eyes at him. "I'd like to see you do better," she challenged, but Will shook his head.

"Unfortunately, you are not training me to shoot," he pointed out. She snorted derisively. "I, on the other hand, am teaching you."

"That's a very convenient excuse," she said. "I would have thought that a large part of teaching someone involved actually demonstrating the task at hand."

"You'd like to see me hit the target?" he asked mildly.

She nodded emphatically. "I would *love* to see you do it."

Will sighed and walked to the shooting line. "Very well," he said. "If you insist."

"Oh, I do!" Maddie told him. She set down her bow and moved to take his place on one side of their improvised shooting range. They were in a cleared space beside their small cabin. The hay bale was suspended from an overhanging tree branch and swung some two meters from the ground. A long cord was attached to it, leading off to one side, and it was here that Will had been standing, pulling on the cord to set the bale swinging like a pendulum to provide a moving target. Maddie retrieved the end of the long cord. The bale, riddled with her arrows, was still swinging, although its momentum was gradually dying away.

The shooting position was approximately thirty meters away, at a right angle to the hay bale's line of movement. Will moved to it and strung his bow, slipping the end into a loop at the back of his boot and bending the two-meter yew shaft over his back and shoulder. He settled himself into position and took an arrow from his belt quiver, fitting the nock securely to the string.

Maddie heaved on the cord and the bale began to swing in a wider arc once more. Will's eyes narrowed as he took in the speed and direction of the swing.

"Turn!" Maddie called, and Will turned to set his back to the target, maintaining the image of the moving bale as he did so. As soon as he was unsighted, Maddie jerked the cord to one side, changing the direction of the swinging target, so that it now moved diagonally rather than merely side to side.

"Turn!" she shouted, and Will spun about, the bow coming up, the arrow drawing back.

He had been on the point of releasing instinctively, with the hay bale's motion ingrained on his memory, when he saw the alteration in its motion. Whereas before it had moved simply from side to side, now it swung in a more complicated motion, moving toward and away from him, as well as laterally. His eyes narrowed as he sized up the new trajectory and he shot.

The arrow zipped across the clearing and thudded into the bale, a hand's breadth away from the center of the red circle. The bale swung wildly off line, its trajectory interrupted by the arrow's impact. Maddie's expectant grin died away.

Will regarded her coolly. "You cheated," he said.

She shrugged irritably. "You always say there's no cheating in war. There's just winning."

"Which I did," he told her. He was feigning annoyance at her but, deep down, he was pleased with her attempt to trick him. It was a very Ranger-ish thing to do, he thought. "Now, would you care to try another shot?" he suggested.

But Maddie was shaking her head before he had finished the invitation. "Oh no, thank you very much," she said.

She knew that if she did, he would ring the changes on her,

making the shot even more difficult. And she wanted to retain her record of six hits from six shots, even though none of them had hit the red circle. She was pleased with her day's results, albeit determined to do better next time they practiced.

Will finally allowed the ghost of a smile. "Very wise," he said, confirming her suspicion of his intentions.

Tug and Bumper were standing by the cabin verandah, interested spectators to their masters' activity. Now Tug, the senior of the two, raised his head and shook his mane, emitting a low rumble of warning. Instantly, the two Rangers looked toward the path through the trees that led from Castle Redmont to their little cabin.

"Someone's coming," Maddie said.

Will nodded. "It's a friend," he said. Tug would have given a different warning if the newcomer had been unknown or an enemy. He half expected it to be Halt, so he was a little surprised when a cloaked figure on a bay mare emerged from the trees and trotted up to the cabin.

"Gilan!" he said. "What brings you to Redmont?"

Will and Maddie began to walk forward to greet the new arrival. The three horses—Tug, Bumper and Gilan's Blaze—all emitted low rumbles of greeting and welcome.

The Ranger Commandant swung down easily from his saddle. Anywhere else, he would wait until he was invited, but the two senior Rangers were old friends, and he knew he was welcome here. He glanced around and took in the hay bale, still swinging from side to side and festooned with arrows.

He nodded approvingly. "Getting in some target practice, I see."

Will glanced back at the shooting range. "Practicing some deflection shooting," he said.

Gilan studied the setup for a few seconds. "Good idea," he said. Will had an inventive mind and was constantly coming up with new challenges for his young apprentice.

Maddie smiled at her Commandant. "Care to try your luck?" she suggested. Her tone was casual, but there was an underlying challenge in her voice.

Gilan sighed inwardly. If he refused, she would manage to bring the matter up repeatedly. His own longbow was slung across his shoulders, and he unslung it now and headed for the shooting range.

"Why not?" he asked. He regarded the bale more closely, taking in the six arrows fringing the red circle and the single shaft inside it, a hand's breadth from the very center.

"Who hit the bull's-eye?" he asked, although he recognized the different markings on the arrows.

"See if you can guess," Will replied.

Gilan grunted and took an arrow from his quiver as Maddie moved to take up the end of the cord. As she hauled on the cord, setting the hay bale swinging, Gilan began to raise his bow. But she stopped him.

"You watch for five seconds, then I tell you to turn away," she said. "Then I'll call on you to turn again and you pivot and shoot."

"From memory?" he queried.

She regarded him with wide-eyed innocence. "If you like," she said.

"Hmmm," Gilan replied. His eyes narrowed as he measured the target's speed and movement, setting it into his memory so that he would see it in his mind's eye, even when his back was turned.

"Turn," Maddie called, and the Commandant turned away from the target. Maddie grinned and prepared to change the bale's movement, but Will stopped her with a quick shake of his head. Gilan might be an old friend, but he was their commanding officer, and it might not be a good idea to trick him into missing. She shrugged and kept the bale swinging on its side-to-side path.

"Turn!" she called.

Gilan spun around, bow coming up. He shot a fraction of a second later, and the arrow slammed into the edge of the hay bale, setting it spinning wildly off course.

Gilan breathed an unseen sigh of relief. It was a good shot, seeing how he was coming into the contest cold and without any prior practice. He assumed Will and Maddie had been shooting for some time. Although she tried to conceal it, Maddie's slightly disappointed air told him that she had expected he would miss clean.

"Good shot," Will told him and gestured toward the cabin. "Come in while I put some coffee on. Maddie," he called to his apprentice, "collect the arrows and attend to Blaze."

"Yes, Will," she replied obediently, and hurried to do as he ordered.

Will turned toward the cabin and dropped a friendly arm over Gilan's shoulders. The Commandant was tall for a Ranger, and Will had to reach up to do so.

"Now, as I was saying, what brings you to Redmont?"

3

GILAN GLANCED BACK TO WHERE MADDIE WAS RECOVERING the arrows from their target practice session.

"I'll wait till Maddie's with us," he said. "That way I won't have to say it all twice."

Will nodded. "That makes sense."

They went inside the little cabin and Will moved to the kitchen area, stirring the embers of the stove and tossing a few more sticks onto the glowing coals. He filled the coffeepot from a jug of fresh water and set it over the flames. While the water was coming to a boil, he took down the jar of freshly ground coffee and set out three mugs.

The water was boiling by the time the door opened and Maddie entered, carrying her quiver and a dozen or so arrows bunched in her left hand. She set them down, separating out four that had damage to their broadheads where they'd skated off trees earlier in the day. She would straighten them later and re-sharpen the edges. She glanced at the two senior Rangers and realized they had been waiting for her to join them.

"So, Gilan," she said, repeating Will's earlier question, "what brings you here—not that we're not delighted to see you, of course," she added with a grin.

Gilan smiled in turn. He liked Maddie. He enjoyed her unfailing good humor and valued her intelligence and skill. Although she was still an apprentice, she had proven her ability and courage on more than one occasion.

"Direwolves," he said, and both Will and Maddie regarded him with surprise. Maddie was the first to speak.

"Direwolves?" she said incredulously. "I thought they were mythical creatures—made up by mothers to scare their children into behaving themselves."

Will raised an eyebrow in her direction. "It would appear your mother had some strange parenting habits," he said, then he turned to Gilan. "All the same, I agree. I thought direwolves were a myth."

Gilan shook his head. "Oh, they're real enough," he said. "Or rather, they *were* real enough. They existed several hundred years ago. It's long been thought that they were extinct."

"Are you saying they're not?" Maddie asked, fascinated.

"I'm saying we've been asked to investigate the possible appearance of a pack of direwolves."

"Whereabouts?" Will asked.

Gilan turned to him to reply. "At a small village in Celtica."

Will leaned back, a distasteful look on his face. "Well, I suppose if they were going to be anywhere," he said, "Celtica would be the place."

"What makes you say that?" Maddie asked him.

"It's a wild, mountainous place, very remote. Roads are bad. Highways are virtually nonexistent, and villages tend to be isolated. There's a lot goes on there that we never hear about.

Communication is poor, and even if it wasn't, the Celts themselves are a secretive people. They tend to resent outsiders knowing too much about what's going on in their country."

Gilan nodded agreement. "I guess that comes with their fascination for mining precious metals. They seem obsessed with the idea that someone will find out where their gold mines are and rob them. Still," he added, "this time they seem to have overcome their reluctance to letting outsiders in on their problems. Queen Madelydd sent a message pigeon to Castle Araluen a few days ago, asking if we'll investigate the reports."

"And what exactly are the reports?" Maddie asked.

Gilan shrugged. "Vague and inconclusive for the most part," he told her. "There have been unsubstantiated sightings of a pack of large canines roaming the mountains." He paused and glanced at Will. "Quite close to the Fissure, as a matter of fact."

Will pursed his lips. It was many years since he had been in that part of Celtica, and it still held bad memories for him.

"Large canines, you say," he said thoughtfully. "Just how large?"

"Some say up to three meters in length, and a meter and a half high at the shoulder. But I'm not sure how accurate they might be. People do tend to exaggerate when they're frightened."

"So we could simply be looking at a pack of wolves—which have grown bigger as the story spread?" Will asked.

"That's the most likely explanation," Gilan admitted. "But there's one detail that concerns me. These beasts have been described with forelegs much longer than their hind legs, so they stand in a kind of hunched-up attitude. Not like normal wolves."

"Did direwolves look like that?" Maddie asked.

Gilan tilted his head. "Nobody's quite sure *what* direwolves looked like. As I said, they haven't been seen in living memory. But a lot of the old tales did describe them as having that configuration."

"And of course, those old tales might well be influencing the way people are describing these beasts," Will observed. "They could be seeing a larger-than-normal wolf, deciding it must be a direwolf and letting their imagination add details that support their supposition."

"That is a definite possibility. But even so, there's another fact that's come up in the last few days. A farmer was killed by one of these creatures."

"You say that's a fact?" Will asked. "Not another rumor?"

Gilan shrugged. "It's as definite as anything we ever hear from Celtica," he said. "But it was mentioned in Queen Madelydd's message. So whether or not it's a direwolf that's responsible, or simply a larger-than-normal wolf, it bears looking into."

"What happened exactly?" Maddie asked.

"The farmer was walking home from the fields with his two brothers when they encountered the beast. It attacked them and they ran for their lives. One of them was too slow, and the wolf—or direwolf if you like—caught him and killed him. The others went back the next day with reinforcements and recovered his body."

"That's not normal behavior for a wolf, is it? I mean, I know they have been known to attack people, but usually they do so in a pack. Have you ever heard of a single wolf attacking a group of men in daylight?"

"It is unusual," Gilan replied. "But it's not impossible."

"Plus, I thought wolves only attacked humans when the

wolves were starving. Yet this one left the body to be recovered the next day."

"True," Gilan told her. "So there's all the more reason for us to investigate. It is extraordinary behavior and we need to look into it."

"The Celts can't do it themselves?" Will asked. "After all, they do have an army, don't they?"

"They do," Gilan replied. "But it's only a small standing army. If war is declared, the reserves are called up, but they predominantly serve as engineers and infantry—most of them are miners, after all. They have no scouts or trackers."

"So we get to pull their chestnuts out of the fire?" Maddie said.

Gilan regarded her coolly. "We have a treaty with them," he said. "It's a mutual defense treaty that says we work together if either country is attacked. They bring skills that we don't have, and vice versa. Queen Madelydd has asked us for help. We can always refuse, of course . . ."

He left the sentence hanging, and Will completed the thought. "But it wouldn't be very diplomatic to do so," he said. "I take it you want us to go and look around below the border?"

His tone left no doubt that he was reluctant to take on the mission. Will had unhappy memories of Celtica, and he had no wish to return to the country. It was barren and rocky and ugly. The people were surly and suspicious.

Gilan, sensing the way he felt, offered a way out. "I could always assign someone else," he said.

Will thought for a few moments, then shook his head. He'd never refused an assignment before, and he wasn't about to start doing so just because he felt uncomfortable about it. That wasn't the way he had been trained or the way he'd behaved over the years, and he was reluctant to set Maddie a bad example. For her part, she was studying him curiously. She had never seen him turn down a mission.

"No. We'll go. We're the closest to the Celtic border. It doesn't make sense to send someone else."

Gilan gave him a quiet nod of gratitude. "Thanks. I appreciate it." He drained the last of his coffee and leaned back in his chair. "I'd suggest you head first to the village where this farmer was killed," he said. "It's called Poddranyth. Ask around, talk to the other farmers who saw this beast and see if you can track it down."

"That makes sense," Will replied. "It sounds like this is at least a definite sighting and not just another rumor. And if we find this creature, whatever it is?"

"If you track it down, kill it. It's a man-killer and we can't leave it roaming around the countryside terrorizing people."

"Odds are, it'll just be a wolf—maybe larger than usual, but a wolf nonetheless."

"True. Although this is Celtica we're talking about," Gilan said.

Will nodded agreement. Strange things did tend to happen in Celtica.

"Can you join us for dinner?" Will asked, changing the subject. "We're going up to the castle to eat with Halt and Pauline."

But Gilan shook his head, smiling. "Jenny would never forgive me if I didn't see her."

Will smiled his understanding. "How do things lie between you two?"

"She won't leave her restaurant and come to Castle Araluen."

"She's an independent woman," Maddie said with a smile.

"True enough," Gilan said. "As a matter of fact, I'm thinking of transferring my headquarters here to Redmont Fief."

Will raised an eyebrow. "How will Cassandra react to that?"

"It shouldn't be too much of a problem. It'll put me closer to you two and to Halt. And Castle Araluen is only two days away. If Cassandra needs me, she can send a message pigeon."

"Have you raised it with her yet?" Will asked.

Gilan shook his head. "I'll do it when I get back."

Will gave him a long look. "Good luck with that," he said.

4

AFTER GILAN HAD LEFT TO VISIT JENNY, MADDIE SAT IN THE afternoon sunshine on the front verandah of the cabin, thinking about their mission. Eventually, she rose and went inside, to where Will was packing for their departure the following morning. She shook her head sadly as she watched him bundling up shirts, underclothes and tights and cramming them any which way into his saddlebags.

"If you folded them neatly, they'd fit much easier," she pointed out.

He grinned at her. It was a conversation they'd had several times before. "But it'd take twice as long that way," he said, as she knew he would.

Giving up, she changed the subject. "I thought I'd go up to the castle and see if George has any information on direwolves," she said.

"Good idea. Give him my regards."

George and Will had grown up together in the Ward, the orphanage that Baron Arald created to care for children of his subjects who had died in service of the Fief. When the time had come to select a career, George had chosen to train as a scribe. Over the next twenty years, he had served in various ways: as an advocate, a linguist and an academic. On a mission to Nihon-Ja, he had saved Horace's life and been wounded by an arrow in doing so. Returning to Redmont, he took the position of castle librarian and researcher.

"I'll meet you in Halt's apartments later," she said. Will nodded distractedly, trying to work out why his spare boots wouldn't fit into his saddlebags. Smiling to herself, Maddie left the cabin, saddled Bumper and headed up the forest path that led to the castle.

The sentries on duty at the drawbridge recognized her and waved her into the courtyard. She left Bumper in the care of a stable boy and entered the central keep tower, where the library was situated.

George was sitting at his desk—a large table covered in manuscripts and volumes of reference material. He looked up and smiled at her as she entered. The library was a large, quiet room on the second floor. The ceilings were high, and the outer wall was lined with tall windows through which light streamed, catching the whirling dust motes in its beams.

George was almost totally bald now, with only a narrow fringe of white hair at the back of his head. The lack of hair made him seem older than he was, but there was still a twinkle in his eyes as he saw the young Ranger entering. George liked Maddie. Most people did.

"Young Maddalena," he exclaimed. He was currently brushing up his Iberian language skills. "Welcome to my dim and dusty abode. Mi casa es su casa. How can I be of service?"

"I wanted to find out about direwolves," Maddie told him.

A knowing look crossed his face. "Ah! You've been told about the events in Celtica, I take it?"

She regarded him with surprise. "How did you know about that?" she asked.

He smiled, tapping his forefinger on the side of his nose in a knowing gesture. She shook her head. George had his own sources of information, and there was little that went on in the Kingdom or its neighbors without his knowledge.

"I have my ways," he said. "And I keep my ears open. I wouldn't be much of a researcher if I didn't."

He rose from behind the table and moved to a crowded bookshelf on the eastern wall, studying the spines of the volumes stacked there before making a selection and pulling it loose. Maddie trailed him to a table and watched as he laid the heavy book down and flicked the pages open.

"Ah, here we are!" he muttered, more to himself than to her. She sat beside him, craning over his shoulder to see the book.

There was an illustration, followed by a small block of text. Maddie raised her eyebrows as she studied the illustration, rendered in fine pen and black ink. It showed a horrendous beast, somewhat wolflike but with forelegs half as long again as the hind legs. This gave the creature a distinctive hunched look as it thrust its head forward to view the ground before it. The head itself was like that of a wolf, with a long snout and huge fangs bared in a snarl. The eyes had been depicted as narrowed, adding to the menacing look of the animal.

To one side was the outline of a normal wolf for size reference. It was one-third the size of the direwolf.

George read the text below the illustration, tracing the words with a forefinger.

"*Direwolf, lupus horribilis, ancient antecedent to common wolf. Possibly mythical. Habitat: Araluen, Celtica, Picta and parts of the western continent."* He glanced up at her. "Hmm, sounds like they got around."

"Except they were possibly mythical," she pointed out.

He nodded and resumed reading. *"Aggressive in nature, carnivorous—"*

"What does that mean?" Maddie interposed.

"Means they ate people," he told her wryly, then continued to quote the text. *"Usually found in small groups of up to half a dozen animals."*

"I wouldn't care to run into half a dozen of those beasts," Maddie said.

George looked at her with a smile. "I wouldn't care to run into one of them," he said. Then, resuming the reading, *"Said to hunt by the light of the full moon . . .* Hmmm, wouldn't pay too much attention to that."

Maddie looked at him curiously. "Why not?"

He pushed his bottom lip out in a skeptical expression. "Smacks a bit too much of myth and legend. A creature that size would need to eat more than three or four days a month. It's more likely that they were seen at the time of the full moon because there was more light then." He returned to the text. *"No sightings in modern times."* He sat back from the table. "And that's all it tells us," he said.

Maddie studied the illustration further. "You'll have to amend your book if it turns out the Celtic farmers are telling the truth," she observed.

George nodded slowly. "Well, if direwolves were going to crop up again, Celtica would be the most likely place. It's wild and largely uninhabited. They could have retreated to the mountains years ago and never been seen."

"That's what Will said." She laid her hand on the illustration. "Mind if I copy this? It might come in handy when we speak to the farmers."

George spread out a hand in permission. "Be my guest. There's paper and pens on my desk if you want them. Bring the book back to me when you've finished."

Maddie spent the next half hour making a copy of the illustration. She was a competent artist, and the result was a fairly accurate depiction of the illustration in the book. Although, she thought, how accurate the original illustration might be was questionable. It would be based on handed-down verbal accounts of direwolves and was liable to be prone to inaccuracies creeping in with each version of the telling—with the usual exaggerations and variations such word-of-mouth accounts suffered from.

When she had finished, she returned the book to George and folded her drawing away into a satchel she carried slung over her shoulder. She thanked him and he smiled at her.

"Take care," he told her. "Even if the thing you're looking for isn't a direwolf, it sounds like a pretty nasty beast."

"I will, George. And thanks for your help." She glanced at the water clock he kept on his desk. "I'd better be going. We're dining with Halt and Pauline."

"I'm sure Halt will have advice on how to deal with a direwolf," George said. "Give my regards to Will."

"I will," she said and headed for the door. She was almost there when George called after her. She turned back.

"What is it?" she asked.

"If you do run into a direwolf, make sure you get a good look at it. And come back to see me with all the details. *Then* we'll amend the book."

5

WILL AND MADDIE RODE OUT THE FOLLOWING MORNING, AFTER dropping Sable up to the castle for Halt and Pauline to look after. Sable always enjoyed staying with Lady Pauline, as she and the elegant courier were in total agreement on how much a dog should be spoiled.

Leaving Castle Redmont, the two Rangers stopped in Wensley village for provisions for the journey.

Will tied the two burlap sacks containing bacon, flour, butter, fresh bread and vegetables on either side of his saddle pommel, and then they struck out to the south.

The southern section of Redmont Fief varied between open farmlands and heavily wooded forest. It was pleasant country, and they rode at a moderate pace through it. As ever when on the move, their senses were alert for any unusual activity in the countryside around them, but this day there was nothing to attract their attention.

Just after midday, they stopped at a tavern in a small village to rest the horses. The tavern keeper bustled nervously around them, making sure they had everything they wanted. His clientele usually consisted of the local farmers and villagers, with an occasional transient traveler. To have two Rangers gracing his establishment was something well and truly out of the ordinary, and several of the locals came to gape at the cloaked figures as they sat enjoying the sunshine and their midday meal.

"May as well save our food stocks for when we need them," Will had said as they were served a savory meat-and-vegetable stew that had been simmering over the fireplace in a large blackened pot. He drained the last of his coffee—they had delved into their own supplies for that as the tavern had only ale and water—and placed a silver coin on the table. The innkeeper hurriedly pushed it back toward him.

"No charge for you, sir," he said. "No charge for the King's Rangers."

Will looked him in the eye and pushed the coin back toward him. "Nonsense," he said. "The food was excellent and the service was friendly. And King's Rangers pay their way."

The man nodded his head gratefully as he accepted the money. In his experience, powerful figures took what they wanted and saw it as their due. The Ranger's sense of fair reward for services rendered was surprising to him.

"You're providing a service," Will told him, "and you deserve to be paid for it. Don't sell yourself—or that excellent stew—short."

"My wife made the stew, sir," the man replied, looking at the silver coin in his hand with delight.

Will nodded gravely. "Then perhaps you should give her the money," he said. "She definitely earned it."

A slightly disappointed look came over the tavern keeper's face. He looked again at the coin, the equivalent of a full night's trading in the tavern. "Perhaps I will," he said doubtfully. He didn't want to set a precedent with his wife. If she got the idea that her cooking was worth more than his ale, it might make life awkward. Will sensed his hesitance.

"Or not," he said, smiling. "I'll leave it to you to decide. Maybe it should just go into general revenue."

He glanced at Maddie as the innkeeper moved away.

"Remember that," he told her. "Don't ever be beholden to any-one." He paused, then added, "Besides, these people have little enough. It's not fair for us to take from them without paying."

She smiled and nodded. It was a lesson that he had taught her many times before, and one he had learned from Halt. They both knew there were some Rangers who accepted free drinks, meals and accommodation. But those Rangers were exceptions to the rule.

They rode on that afternoon. The countryside was becom-ing progressively less settled, the farms and cultivated fields fewer and farther between. By late afternoon, they were in thick wood-land, following a narrow road through the trees. Reaching a small stream, Will called a halt.

"Might as well make camp here for the night," he said. "I doubt we'll see too many inns from here on."

They found a small clearing away from the road and made their camp. It was a simple enough matter. The weather was good and they wouldn't need tents. While Maddie cleared a space for a fire and surrounded it with a circle of rocks, Will made his way to the small stream. The water was clear and fast-running, and as he stood on the bank he could see signs of trout rising to take insects from the surface, leaving widening rings on the water to mark their presence. There seemed to be a lot of them, and in a remote spot like this it was unlikely that they had been bothered by fishermen before.

He looked around the calf-length grass and saw small grass-hoppers flitting among the stalks. Quickly, he gathered half a dozen of the little insects, wrapping them carefully in a handkerchief and stowing it in his pocket. Then he drew his saxe and cut a long, whippy branch from one of the nearby trees. He took a length of waxed cord from the small satchel he carried over his shoulder and attached it to the end of the two-meter branch. On the free end, there was a small hook, and he carefully threaded one of the small, wriggling grasshoppers onto it, then lowered it into the water, letting the current take it downstream to where he had just seen a fish rise.

Almost immediately, there was a small flurry in the water and the line went tight, pulling the improvised rod into a curve as the trapped fish struggled against it. He reached up to the tip of the pole and took hold of the line, drawing it gently in to the bank and bringing the fish with it.

In less than five minutes, he had four fish lying on the grass at his feet. He knocked them over the head with the hilt of his saxe to stop their frantic struggling for oxygen.

He untied his fishing line and rolled it up again, then scooped up the fish and headed back to the campsite, where Maddie had started a fire.

"Good work," he said.

She eyed the four plump fish that he dropped beside the fireplace. "I might say the same," she replied.

The fire was burning too high to cook the fish, so he put a blackened pot of water on the flames to boil and added four small potatoes to it. The pot bubbled merrily and the lid clattered against the escaping steam.

When the flames had died down sufficiently, he raked the glowing coals together and placed a heavy-based skillet on top of them, dropping a large pat of butter into the hot pan. While it melted, he dredged the fish in flour seasoned with salt and pepper, then laid them gently into the pan, where they sizzled as the skin browned.

After five minutes, he turned them carefully, cooked them for several more minutes, then laid them on a clean patch of grass. The potatoes were soft, so he sliced them into narrow strips and put the strips in the pan to brown. Maddie brought their plates to the fireside, and he placed two fish and some of the potato strips on each.

She sniffed appreciatively. "Smells good," she said.

He grinned at her. "Your turn to cook tomorrow."

Holding the fish down with his saxe, he gripped the tail and carefully raised the backbone away from the pink meat until he had two fillets, free of bones, on his plate. Maddie had less patience and she attacked the fish, flaking the meat away from the backbone and eating eagerly, pausing occasionally to remove small bones from her mouth.

They finished the meal as the sun finally set, and Maddie made coffee, then took the plates and pans to the stream to wash them.

They sat by the fire in companionable silence, finishing their coffee. Finally, Will heaved a contented sigh.

"There may be a better life than this," he said, "but I have no idea what it might be."

Despite the early hour, Maddie yawned. It had been a long day in the saddle, with only a brief stop at the inn to have lunch.

"Will we keep watch tonight?" she asked.

Will looked around the surrounding trees and shook his head. "No need. The horses will warn us if anyone happens by," he said.

All the same, they extinguished the fire—the small comfort it provided wasn't worth revealing their presence—and, as was their practice, moved away from the clearing into the bushes to spread their blankets. The horses stood watch over them as they rolled out their groundsheets, wrapped themselves in their cloaks and lay down to sleep, heads resting on their saddles.

For a few minutes, Maddie lay, warm in her cloak and comfortable on the soft grass, listening to the sounds of the forest at night. As the campsite grew silent, the nocturnal birds and insects resumed their nightly movement. She was interested by the fact that Will, who was an enthusiastic snorer when he slept in their cabin, slept silently when he was in the field. She guessed there was a part of his mind that was still awake and in control.

Then she closed her eyes and dropped off into a deep, dreamless sleep.

6

THEY AWOKE EARLY THE FOLLOWING DAY, BREAKFASTING ON fried bacon and the fresh bread they had carried with them. The morning was chilly and they huddled over the warmth of the rekindled fire, sipping their coffee. Finally, Will tossed the dregs into the fire and kicked dirt over the embers.

"Time to go," he said, and they saddled their horses and broke camp, riding out of the trees to the narrow road they had been following.

As they continued to ride south, the landscape gradually changed. The thick forest gave way to open ground, and the rich soil slowly transformed to rocky, sandy terrain as they wended their way uphill. The mountains of Celtica rose up on the horizon, towering over them, capped with white snow. What trees they passed were stunted, windblown and far between, and their horses' hooves clattered unevenly on the rocky ground underfoot.

Around midday, they crested a rise. The mountains seemed much closer now. A long, sweeping downhill slope lay ahead of them, and beyond it, the ground rose again to a rocky ridgeline. Will pointed to it.

"Celtica," he said.

There was a small stone building huddled beside the road, with a hinged pole forming a barrier to traffic. They urged their horses forward. As they came closer, they could see several figures gathered around the barrier pole, watching them intently.

Will drew rein when they were a few meters from the barrier, searching the small group for the senior man. None of them wore insignia of any kind, although all of them were in half armor and armed with short swords and spears. Finally, a bearded soldier, who seemed to be older than the others, moved forward into the middle of the road.

"Who goes there?" he demanded brusquely. Maddie thought it was a pointless challenge. It was obvious they were a pair of Rangers. Nonetheless, Will replied politely.

"Araluen King's Rangers, responding to a summons from Queen Madelydd of the Celts," he announced.

The border guard eyed him truculently. "Names?" he asked.

Will sighed, shifting in his saddle. "Will Treaty," he replied, and indicating Maddie, "and Madelyn Altman." He used Horace's surname, as it wasn't as widely known in Celtica as the royal family's and it concealed the fact that Maddie was the daughter of the crown princess of Araluen.

"Never heard of you," the guard replied. "What's your business in Celtica?"

Will eyed him for a few seconds, then spoke again. "I'm afraid that's none of your concern," he told the man. "We've come in response to a summons from your queen, and if she wants you to know about it, I'm sure she would have told you."

The guard frowned, checking quickly to see that his men were still close at hand. "We've had no notification," he said.

Will shrugged. "Then I assume the queen *doesn't* want you

to know about it," he replied. He gathered up his reins and began to turn Tug's head back the way they had come. "I imagine you'll be hearing from her when I put in my report and tell her you've turned us away. Come on, Maddie."

He urged Tug around and began to walk him away from the border crossing, back to Araluen. Maddie waited until he'd cleared the way, then followed. She turned back in her saddle and saw the look of alarm on the guard's face as he realized he could be in trouble.

"Just a moment!" the man called after them.

Will allowed Tug to take several more paces, then checked him. But he remained facing away from the border crossing.

"Come back. Maybe I was a little hasty," the guard called. The nervousness in his voice was all too evident. When he saw Will making no move to turn back, he added: "Please?"

Will touched Tug with his heel, and the shaggy little horse turned and headed back to the border crossing. Maddie, hiding a smile, followed suit on Bumper. Will stopped just short of the barrier and looked down at the guard.

"You weren't hasty," he told the man. "You were downright rude. Last I heard, Araluen and Celtica were allies and our borders are open. Therefore, you have no reason to bar us from entering your country. Or have you been told differently?"

The guard dropped his gaze and shuffled his feet awkwardly. "No, sir. No, I haven't been told differently. My apologies, sir," he mumbled.

Will said nothing, letting the silence between them stretch out. Finally, he replied. "Very well. Remember it when the next travelers arrive at your border. What's your name?"

"Rhys, sir. Rhys Davies," the guard told him.

"Rank?" Will asked.

"Corporal, sir."

"I'll bear it in mind when I come to write my report," Will told him.

The guard turned quickly to one of his men, standing by the counterweight on the shorter end of the barrier pole. "Gwynn, raise that barrier now for the Rangers!"

The other man leaned his weight on the pole, swiveling it upward and allowing Will and Maddie to cross into Celtica. Will nodded curtly to the corporal as he passed. Maddie urged Bumper after Tug and followed for a few meters, then, as the road widened, pulled up beside Will.

"What was that all about?" she asked.

Will shrugged. "I can't stand petty tyrants like that. Give them a little authority and they turn into the worst kind of bullies. He's angry and he plans to take it out on anyone who wants to cross."

"What's he angry about? We didn't do anything to annoy him."

Will shook his head. "Not at us. Just at life in general. As you know, the Celts have a small army, and it's largely comprised of conscripts. Every Celt male has to serve six months as a soldier. It's only a short term, so there are never very many of them, but they resent having to do it. There's been no war in recent years, and they've grown complacent. They feel there's no need for an army."

"People often feel that—until there's trouble," Maddie observed.

Will nodded. "That's right. And by then, it's too late. But men like Corporal Davies feel it's a waste of their valuable time.

They'd rather be grubbing for gold and silver in their dark little mines."

"That seems to be the principal interest of the Celts." Maddie smiled.

"True. They're a surly, unsmiling lot. It sometimes seems to me that they've all got a permanent chip on their shoulders. They want the world to leave them alone while they scrabble away underground."

"But you haven't been to Celtica for years, have you?" she asked.

He shook his head. "No. But I've seen plenty of them at councils where the treaty has been renewed. And Halt has told me a lot about them as well. According to him, they have two interests: mining and brigandage. They're either mining for gold or stealing it."

"They sound like fun people," Maddie said.

Will shrugged and remained silent. The character and behavior of the Celtic people was a source of annoyance for him.

At noon, they found a clearing in the rocky ground beside the road and stopped to rest and water the horses. Maddie foraged for firewood, gathering deadfalls from the small, stunted trees that grew among the rocks, and boiling water for coffee. They ate flatbread and dried meat and fruit.

After a short rest, they resumed their journey. The road, such as it was, was narrow and winding, climbing beside a steep cliff to one side and a rocky, dizzying drop on the other. Will consulted his map as they rode. Navigation in Celtica was relatively simple: there was only one main road for the first twenty kilometers, then it forked into two.

"We'll stay on this road for another six or seven kilometers," he told her. "Then we fork right to go to Poddranyth."

"How far is that?" she asked.

"Not far. We should make it by nightfall."

"That's good. I wasn't looking forward to another night camping out. Those clouds are looking ominous," she replied. Above them, the wind was driving dark-looking rain clouds across the sky.

Will glanced up at them and grunted. "It always rains in Celtica."

She smiled at him. "You're a bundle of positive feelings about this country, aren't you?"

He smiled back, in spite of himself. "Sorry. It's just my previous visit left a bad taste in my mouth." He let his gaze wander across the deep valley beside them. "At least this time we don't have to contend with Wargals."

She regarded him curiously. "What were they like?" she asked. "They were before my time."

He paused a moment before answering. "They were dreadful creatures," he said eventually. "At least, while they were under Morgarath's mind control. Left to their own devices, they were harmless enough. But he had them focused on killing and sub-jugating the Celts, and they were so single-minded about it they were terrifying. I had nightmares about them for years after."

"You?" she said, surprised. Will was so confident, so self-reliant and so capable, she couldn't imagine him having nightmares about anything.

But he nodded. "Oh yes. They were ghastly-looking creatures. They walked sort of half upright, with their knuckles trailing on the ground. Think of a cross between a wolf and a bear. Heavyset and powerful, with a long muzzle and large canine fangs. And they were focused totally on doing Morgarath's bidding." He shuddered theatrically at the thought of them. "They had a kind of mindless evil about them that could chill your blood."

He closed his eyes for a second and heard again the toneless, rhythmic chanting that Wargals used to make when they were on the move. Then he opened them again as he and Maddie rounded a bend in the mountain road and saw what was waiting for them, some fifty meters ahead.

"Oh no," he said quietly. "Looks like we're about to encounter Celtica's second-most-popular pastime."

7

THE ROAD AHEAD WAS BLOCKED BY A ROUGH BARRICADE OF rocks, standing about waist high. There was a gap in the center, closed by a heavy beam of timber positioned as a gate. Three men stood before the barricade. They wore mismatched items of armor over their rough working clothes. One had a mail shirt that seemed far too big for him, another wore a leather breastplate and the third was dressed in a leather tunic sewn with small brass plates set close together to provide some protection against knife or sword thrusts, and a flat-topped pot helmet with a broad nasal projecting down to cover his nose.

The nasal was too wide for his face and gave him a slightly cross-eyed look. He was armed with a sword—a heavy broadsword with an extended hilt that would allow him to use it two-handed, although with what amount of skill was questionable. The others carried heavy, studded cudgels.

The helmet wearer stepped forward and held up his left hand in a gesture commanding them to stop. He held the sword, point down, in his right hand. It was an unwieldy weapon, and it appeared badly balanced and clumsy.

"Here we go again," muttered Will.

Maddie glanced at him curiously. "How do you mean?"

He sighed in exasperation as he allowed Tug to take a few

more paces before bringing him to a stop. "Your father and I had
to put up with this sort of nonsense when we were here before,"
he said. "We were camped for the night and two raggedy-pants
bandits like this decided it might be a good idea to rob us."

"What happened?" Maddie asked. "I haven't heard this story."

"We were practicing with drill swords and didn't hear them
coming. Then Gilan arrived and they didn't hear him. As I recall, he suggested that Horace might complete his sword practice
with one of the robbers as a partner. Your dad gave him a very
unpleasant whacking." A faint smile touched his mouth at the
memory. "Turns out that robbing us wasn't such a good idea
after all. Have you got your sling handy?"

Maddie nodded as she unwound the harmless-looking weapon
from her wrist.

"Then keep it ready."

He urged Tug forward again with a slight pressure of his
knees. The helmeted man raised his left hand again and Will
stopped once more. They were now only ten meters apart.

"That's far enough!" the bandit called. His tone was threatening and unfriendly. "We are the guardians of the road!" At the
same time, his two companions brandished their cudgels, as if to
emphasize his statement.

Will raised an eyebrow and looked at the rough, unpaved
surface of the road beneath Tug's hooves. "In that case, let me
offer you my congratulations on a good job," Will said.

The man frowned, puzzled by the words and the positive
tone behind them. "Congratulations?" he repeated. "What are
you talking about?"

Will gestured to the road. "Well, as far as I can see, the road
hasn't gone anywhere, so you must have been guarding it well."

The swordsman's face reddened with anger as he realized Will was mocking him. "Don't play word games with me, graybeard!" he shouted.

Will pursed his lips as he considered the man's words. "Graybeard? That's a little excessive, isn't it? I mean, *grizzled*, perhaps. *Distinguished*, certainly. But *graybeard*? I'm not sure I accept that."

"I don't give a moldy fig if you accept it or not! I'll have your purse! And I'll have it now!" The man raised the sword in a threatening gesture. Then it obviously became too heavy to maintain the pose and he let the point drop back to the road.

If he had noticed the longbows slung across the travelers' shoulders, he gave no sign. But longbows weren't considered a weapon in Celtica. If they were used at all, it was for hunting, not fighting, and they certainly didn't have the massive power of Will's eighty-pound-draw bow. So to all appearances, the man and girl before him were unarmed.

"Maddie," Will said in a casual tone, keeping his eyes on the belligerent Celt before him, "would you oblige me by putting a dent in that man's silly-looking hat?"

Abruptly, Maddie stood in her stirrups, gripping Bumper's barrel-like body with her thighs and knees and turning slightly side-on to the startled robber. She extended her right arm behind her, letting the loaded sling drop to full length, then whipped it up and over, following through as she released so that her hand pointed straight at her target.

The self-styled guardians of the road heard a brief whizzing sound, then a loud *CLANG!* as the lead slug slammed into the center of the helmet, just above the nasal. The swordsman staggered back, the heavy sword falling from his hand and ringing metallically on the roadbed, then he fell as well, stretching his length in the dust and rocks and moaning softly.

His companions gaped at him in shock, not sure what they had just witnessed, uncertain as to what had struck him down. Fearfully, they began to back away.

"That's enough!" Will's voice cracked like a whip. "Stand where you are!"

They did as he ordered, their eyes flicking uncertainly between him and Maddie, who remained upright in the stirrups, another lead slug loaded into her sling, the twin thongs dangling behind her, swinging gently to and fro as she prepared to cast again. Slowly, awareness dawned on the two bandits as they realized what had just happened.

"Now, clear that mess off the road," Will ordered, and the men moved uncertainly toward the barrier. "Get a move on!" he snapped, and they moved with greater speed, but still stood, uncertain what to do with the rocks and timber that formed the barricade. Will gestured toward the drop on his right.

"Sling it all down there!" he ordered.

The bandits bent and began to throw the rocks into the void below them. The sound of the rocks crashing and bouncing down the slope came back to them as they worked. Maddie remained standing in her stirrups. Will sat in his saddle, his hands folded on the pommel in front of him as the barricade was slowly consigned to the void. Eventually, the way was clear, aside from the prone figure of the helmeted man, who lay groaning and semiconscious.

"Him too," Will told them.

They moved to grasp the man by the elbows and knees and began to drag him toward the edge of the drop.

"Don't throw him over!" Will snapped. "Just get him out of the way. Set him by the roadside."

Relieved that they weren't expected to hurl their comrade into the depths of the valley, they laid him down on the edge of the road. He groaned continuously as they moved him, his eyes shut.

"Strip off his boots and pants. Yours too," the Ranger ordered. They obeyed hesitantly.

Will gestured toward the steep drop. "Over they go," he ordered, and the men, clad only in their upper clothes and underwear, threw their boots and trousers into empty space.

"Your weapons as well," Will told them, and they retrieved their cudgels from the road, along with the broadsword, and sent them flying into space. The sword could be heard clanging from rock to rock as it bounced end over end down the valley.

"Now get out of here," Will ordered, and they began to shuffle off down the road. "Oy!" he called, stopping them. They peered back at him. "Take that piece of rubbish with you!" Will commanded, pointing at the dazed man by the roadside.

They scurried to do his bidding, grunting with effort as they lifted their semiconscious friend and began to crab-walk away, carrying him between them.

Will watched them go and sighed. "What a rabble," he said, more to himself than to Maddie.

She finally subsided into her saddle, winding the sling around her wrist and closing the shot pouch at her belt. "You always tell them to take off their boots and pants," she remarked with a smile.

Will nodded. "It stops them robbing travelers," he said. "They can't walk comfortably or quickly with no boots, and they're less frightening without their pants."

"I don't know about that." Maddie grinned. "Did you see the

state of their underpants?" She shuddered theatrically. In truth, she was only making idle conversation. She had used the same ploy on robbers herself in the past and knew the thinking behind it.

"Let's get a move on," Will said. "We've wasted enough time here as it is."

They urged their horses forward. A few minutes later, they overtook the two robbers, struggling with the burden of their comrade. Hearing the horses behind them, they dropped him unceremoniously onto the road and scurried for shelter in the rocks to their left. Will and Maddie rode around the groaning figure and continued on their way, ignoring the two men cowering among the rocks.

"Nice friends," Maddie observed.

Will looked sidelong at her. "You expected anything different?" he asked.

She didn't reply.

They rode on as the sun sank lower behind the mountains, casting long, distorted shadows on the road ahead of them. After some time, they came to the fork in the road Will had mentioned. He gestured to the right.

"We go this way," he said, and they angled off the main highway onto the side trail, though there was little to tell between the two roads. The highway, so-called, was as narrow and as unfinished as the side road.

Twenty minutes later, they rounded the edge of a large bluff and reined in. Across the valley, accessible by a solid-looking stone bridge, was a small collection of low houses, huddled into the hillside, seeming to take shelter from the ever-present wind.

"Poddranyth," said Will.

8

THE BRIDGE WAS A NARROW, HUMPBACKED AFFAIR WITH NO balustrade on either side. Gingerly, Maddie set Bumper for the middle and began to cross. The nimble little horse showed no sign of concern as he trotted forward, and she peered to the side, looking down into the depths of the chasm, where a river could be heard rushing on its way. In the gathering twilight, she could make out the white foam of its passage.

She let out a sigh of relief as the horse stepped onto the far bank. Will followed her, smiling at her obvious discomfort.

"There's nothing to worry about," he told her. "If there's one thing the Celts are good at, it's building in stone."

She made no reply. *It would have been good to hear that before we crossed*, she thought.

It began to rain as they turned toward the little village—a light, persistent drizzle that formed in small drops on their cloaks where the natural lanolin in the wool stopped them from soaking in. Bumper shook his mane and shivered his muscles to rid himself of the water.

Poddranyth was a collection of around thirty small houses set in several uneven rows on the left side of the road. They were all built in stone, with the majority roofed in the same material, split into thin tiles. Half a dozen were thatched, and the thatching was looking worse for wear. About two-thirds of the way along the village, one building was larger than the others. A wooden sign swung outside its doorway, depicting a mug of ale in peeling, discolored paintwork. Maddie was used to taverns with colorful signs and names—such as the Red Deer, the Silver Crown or the King's Head. This simple, prosaic way of identifying the village tavern was well in keeping with the dour nature of the Celts she had witnessed so far.

"People of few words," she muttered to herself as they reined in before the single-story building. There were two small windows in the wall facing them, set either side of the door. They were covered in scraped oilcloth and she could make out the light behind them, although she couldn't see the interior. A low buzz of conversation could be heard inside.

"No stable," Will remarked. "I imagine the locals come on foot."

They swung down and untied their oiled tarpaulin horse covers from behind their saddles, draping them over Tug and Bumper to protect them from the rain. In truth, the horses could have managed without them. Their shaggy coats provided good protection from the weather. But there was no point in their being more uncomfortable than they had to be. The two horses moved so that they were facing away from the wind. There was no need to restrain them. Ranger horses didn't wander off.

Will stepped to the door, opened it and led the way in. Even though he was a relatively short man, he had to stoop below the overhanging eave and the low door lintel.

The conversation inside the large room stopped as they entered. The room was filled with smoke from a coal fire at one end, with an inadequate chimney that appeared to send most of the smoke from the fire back into the room. There were eight or nine small tables, with low stools beside them, set throughout the room. On the wall opposite the door, the bar was formed by three long planks supported by empty barrels. The tavern keeper, a solidly built man wearing a leather apron, presided behind it. He was accompanied by a middle-aged woman, most likely his wife. On the shelf behind them was a row of wooden mugs. A tapped ale barrel stood on its side at one end of the bar. There were two oil lanterns set in the back wall, and single candles burned on the tables. A dozen people were present, in groups of twos and threes, seated at the tables. They were all turned toward the doorway to view the newcomers.

"Close the door," one called, and Maddie swung the door shut on its leather hinges.

"Greetings to all here," Will said, the traditional greeting on entering a public place. Nobody responded, and he led Maddie through the watching, silent faces to the bar. The tavern keeper reached behind him for two wooden ale mugs and placed them on the bar.

"Did you want ale?" he asked.

Will paused to throw back the hood of his cloak, sending a small shower of droplets onto the floor. "Do you have coffee?" he asked.

The barman replaced the mugs on the shelf and looked sidelong at his wife, who shrugged.

"I can make a pot," she said, without enthusiasm.

Will smiled at her but evoked no response. "We'll have coffee then," he said. "And a jar of honey if you have it."

She nodded and moved to a room behind the bar—presumably

the kitchen. Will turned away from the bar and surveyed the main room and the dozen pairs of eyes that were still fastened on him and Maddie. Slowly, the occupants began to resume their interrupted conversations, as they decided they had seen all they needed to see of the newcomers.

Will looked back at the barman. "Is there anything to eat?" he asked.

The man shrugged. "Bread and cheese. Nothing hot yet."

"Bread and cheese it is," Will replied. His eyes were smarting from the smoky atmosphere in the room. The barman turned away to the shelf behind the bar and placed a round of yellow cheese and a small cottage loaf of bread on a platter. He rattled it down on the bar in front of Will, who smiled his thanks.

"We're looking for the ap-Jones brothers," Will said. "Would they be here at all?"

Instantly, the renewed mutter of conversations in the room went still again. Will, watching intently, saw several eyes go to a pair of men sitting to one side, away from the door. They, alone among those present, remained looking steadfastly away from the two Rangers.

"What would you be wanting with them?" the barman asked, his tone challenging.

Will shrugged. "We mean them no harm," he said. "We simply want to talk."

There was a long pause while the barman studied Will, trying to gauge if he was any level of threat to the ap-Jones brothers. Unable to come to a decision, he temporized.

"They may not want to talk to you," he said.

"Then that's their right, of course," Will said evenly. "But as I said, we mean them no harm."

The impasse was broken by the return of the barman's companion, bearing a blackened coffeepot, two mugs and a small jar of honey on a wooden tray. She set them on the bar in front of Will and glanced curiously at her husband, feeling the tension between him and the cloaked newcomer.

"They want to speak to the ap-Jones brothers," he said, sensing her unspoken question.

Maddie was watching the woman closely. She saw her eyes flit to the two men at the far table, then quickly switch back to the barman.

"What do they want with them?" she asked.

Will answered before her husband could speak. "We simply want to talk to them about the creature that attacked their brother," he said.

The woman's eyes narrowed in suspicion. "How do you know about that? You're not from round here, are you?"

"No, we're from Araluen. But word gets around. We're here to help."

She peered more closely at him, taking in the mottled cloak and the massive longbow slung over his shoulder.

"From Araluen, you say?" she asked.

Will nodded. "That's right."

"You're Rangers, aren't you?" she continued.

Again Will nodded.

She pursed her lips thoughtfully. "There were Rangers here years ago," she said. "During the troubles with the Lord of Rain and Night. I was just a girl at the time." She turned to her husband. "They were good people," she said. "Good fighters too."

Her husband studied the two cloaked figures with renewed interest. He pointed at Maddie. "She's a girl," he said doubtfully.

Maddie sighed. It was a reaction she was used to and it always rankled.

"She's my apprentice," Will said.

The barman and his wife exchanged a glance and seemed to come to a decision.

"I suppose we could let the ap-Jones brothers know you want to talk," said the barman. "We'll let them decide whether to do so or not."

"Will you be staying in the village?" the woman asked.

Will looked around the low-ceilinged, smoky room. "Do you have rooms?"

She shook her head. "Not here. But the widow Maeve provides beds for travelers. Her place is three doors down." She indicated the direction with a nod of her head. "Nothing fancy, but it's clean."

"That'll be fine," Will told her, picking up the platter of bread and cheese. He nodded toward the tray with the coffeepot and mugs, and Maddie took it. They turned away from the bar and he led the way to a table beside the two men they had marked out as the ap-Jones brothers. The muted conversations throughout the room began again as they sat and began to eat and drink. The cheese was surprisingly good, sharp-tasting and moist. The bread was coarse but fresh-baked. The coffee was indifferent, but at least it was hot.

Maddie glanced at the two men sitting at the adjacent table. She opened her mouth to speak, but Will shook his head, and she took another bite of bread instead. As she did, the two men rose abruptly and made their way toward the door. Maddie followed them with her eyes. She saw the older of the two exchange a look with the barman and give a slight nod before going out. The candles on the tables flickered in the wind as the door opened, then steadied as it closed behind them. She leaned toward Will.

"You know that was them, don't you?" she said in a low voice.

He nodded. "Patience," he said quietly. "They'll have their reasons for not wanting to talk in public." He poured himself another half cup of coffee. "Now eat up, and we'll go find the widow Maeve."

9

THEY FINISHED THE SIMPLE MEAL IN SILENCE, AWARE THAT they were being constantly scrutinized by the others in the room. Will reached out for the coffeepot and tested its weight. He judged there was perhaps a cup left in it and hesitated, then shook his head and put it back down. The coffee wasn't good enough for another cup. He gathered the platters, mugs and pot onto the tray and rose.

"Let's go," he said, and Maddie stood as well. They crossed to the bar, and he placed the tray in front of the barman. "How much do I owe?" he asked.

The barman thought for a few seconds. "Six coppers," he said.

Will counted the money from his purse, placing it on the bar beside the tray. "Is there a stable anywhere in the village where we can put our horses?" he asked.

The barman nodded. "Maeve has a small barn behind her cottage," he replied. "They'll be fine there."

Pulling their cloaks closer around them, the two Rangers headed for the door and stepped out into the cold, misty rain. Bumper and Tug greeted them with raised heads and a low, warning rumble. Will's hand went to the hilt of his saxe as two dark figures detached themselves from the shelter of the over-hanging roof eave a few meters from the door.

"You won't be needing that," Dai said, and Will relaxed. The man's tone was nervous but not threatening. All the same, he kept his hand near the hilt of the razor-sharp weapon, and he saw that Maddie was equally ready.

"Come with us," Dai said, nodding his head down the narrow main street of the village.

Will gestured to the horses, standing watching the exchange, their ears pricked and alert. "What about our horses?" he asked.

"Mam's cottage has a toolshed behind. They'll be fine in there." He turned and began to walk away, in the direction opposite to where the barman had said Maeve's cottage lay.

Will glanced at Maddie and nodded. Then he clicked his fingers for Tug to follow and set out after the two Celts.

"Bumper, come," Maddie said quietly.

The little procession headed south, passing several houses, then the two Celts turned right into a narrow lane, leading the way to a second row of homes set on a small street parallel to the main road. The houses here were set farther apart. Dai and Gryff stopped at one and indicated a small shelter behind it.

"Your horses can go in there," Dai said. "Bring your bedding. You can stay by our fire tonight."

It was a tight fit in the shed, but the roof was good, and it was dry inside and sheltered from the wind. They unsaddled the horses, rubbed them down with their saddle blankets and spread the blankets and their tarpaulin covers to dry.

Gryff squeezed in through the door as they were looking after the horses and placed a bucket of fresh water on the ground.

Will nodded his thanks, and Maddie set the bucket between the horses. Tug drank first, then moved aside to make room for Bumper.

Will doled out grain from a bag tied to Tug's saddle and put it in the two feed bags. The horses munched noisily. Finally, satisfied that their horses were settled, Will and Maddie picked up their bedrolls and followed the two Celts back to the front door of the little cottage. Dai ushered them in, and they stooped under the low lintel and went inside.

It was warm and smoky in the interior. The cottage was divided into two rooms, with a sleeping loft at one end of the larger of the two. There was a substantial fireplace at the opposite end, with cooking utensils hanging from hooks and a swiveling arm that could hold a pot over the flames of the fire. There was a blackened pot hanging from it now, and a savory smell filled the room. In the center of the room was a wooden table and four stools—the only furnishings in the room.

A curtained doorway led into a second, smaller room, and as they watched, it was swept aside and a woman stepped in to join them.

She was small and gray-haired, but she held herself erect. Her face was lined and her hair was tied back in a tight bun behind her head. Her gray eyes studied them intently as they hesitated inside the door. Then she gestured for them to come toward the fire.

"Come in. Make yourselves warm," she said. "Welcome to our home."

The Rangers moved closer to the fire, shedding their cloaks, bows and quivers and placing their bedrolls on the flagstone floor. Will glanced at the table, seeing it set for five people.

"You were expecting us?"

She nodded. "Young Rhiannon said her mother vouched for you. Said you were people we could trust," she replied.

Maddie cocked her head to one side. "Rhiannon?" she queried.

The older woman looked at her for several seconds, then replied, "The tavern keeper's daughter. Her mother sent her out the back door to warn me."

Maddie nodded her understanding. The girl must have been in the kitchen area of the tavern. Will stepped closer to the glowing coals of the fire. The heat was most welcome after the windy, drizzling weather outside.

"I'm Will Treaty, of Araluen," he told her. "And this is Maddie, my apprentice."

"You're Rangers," the woman stated, and Will nodded.

The woman looked at Maddie with renewed interest. "Didn't know there were girl Rangers," she said. Before Maddie could react with her usual long-suffering sigh, the woman redeemed herself with her next words. "Still, no reason why there shouldn't be. Girls are generally quicker on the uptake than boys."

Maddie smiled in surprise. Instinctively, she liked the gray-eyed Celt woman.

"I'm Glenys Jones," the woman said. "And these are my sons, Gryff and Dai."

The two men, who had been standing back while their mother led the conversation, nodded their heads in greeting.

Will smiled. "We thought you might be," he said, and when the Celts looked puzzled, he explained, "When we mentioned you in the tavern, everybody looked your way."

"That would be right," said Glenys. "It's difficult to keep anything secret in this village."

Maddie smiled at her. "It's the same in any small community," she said. "Everyone tends to know your business."

"Aye, that's correct," Glenys agreed. "But in Poddranyth, that can be dangerous."

Maddie raised her eyebrows in surprise. "Dangerous?" she repeated. "How so?"

"There are dark forces at work in these mountains," Glenys told her. "And it doesn't do to discuss them in public. That's why my boys didn't want to be seen talking to you in the tavern. You never know who might be listening. There are spies everywhere."

"And who are they spying for?" Will asked.

Glenys held his gaze for several seconds, judging to see if his question was a cynical one. Eventually, she seemed assured that his curiosity was genuine.

"For Arazan," she told him. "She's the source of all evil in this area. It's she who has trained a pack of direwolves—one of which killed my boy Owen."

Maddie and Will exchanged quick glance. "Direwolves?" Will queried. "They're extinct, if they ever existed at all."

"Oh, they exist all right. And they're not extinct," Glenys replied, with some heat. "We should know. The boys saw one." She gestured toward her two sons, who were watching the exchange keenly. They both nodded.

Maddie reached into the satchel that hung over her shoulder and produced the drawing she had copied in the Castle Redmont library. She placed it on the table in front of the two farmers, who leaned forward for a closer look.

"Did it look like this?" she asked.

Gryff looked at Dai, deferring to his older brother. After a long pause, Dai replied uncertainly.

"Pretty much," he said. "Not exactly. The one we saw had a longer muzzle."

Maddie glanced down at the sketch. She tapped her fingers on the creature's elongated front legs—perhaps the most distinctive feature of the ancient beast.

"Was it reared up at the front like this?" she asked and both men nodded immediately.

"Aye," said Dai. He looked up at her. "This was pretty much the way it looked, although, as I say, not exactly."

"How did this Arazan woman come to raise a pack of these animals?" Will asked Glenys.

The woman shrugged. "How she does everything. She's in touch with evil forces. Some say she has the gift of farsight, and she can tell when people are talking about her. It may be so, but she also has spies in the village who report back to her—as Alun ap-Alwyn learned to his peril, not two months ago."

"What happened to him? Who is he?" Will asked.

"He *was* a miner," Glenys told him, emphasizing the past tense. "He'd spoken out about Arazan. Her direwolves had been raiding farms and taking animals in the area, and he was trying to raise the villagers to band together and put an end to it. But one morning he was found in his cottage, sitting at his table, eyes wide-open and dead as a stone. There wasn't a mark on him. He'd been struck dead."

"And you say Arazan did this?" Will asked.

"I know Arazan did it," Glenys said firmly, and her two sons muttered in agreement.

"But how?" Maddie asked. "Did anyone see her in the village?"

"No. But she wouldn't need to be there in person. She has powers. She's a necromancer."

Maddie sat back, puzzled. The word was unknown to her. She looked at Will. "A necromancer? What in the world is that?" she asked.

Will looked hard at Glenys before he answered. There was no sign of hysteria or irrational fear there. The woman was calm and confident that what she said was true.

"It's someone who tries to make contact with the dead," he said quietly.

10

"So, tell us more about this Arazan person," Will said. "Where did she come from?"

"She arrived here several years ago," Glenys replied. She was watching him carefully, to see if he was humoring her or if he believed what she was saying. "She came from the south originally—I don't know where. She just arrived one day and took over an abandoned cottage in Tenruath—a village about eight kilometers from here. Word soon got around that she was conducting unholy rituals late at night. They said she was trying to raise the spirit of the Lord of Rain and Night."

"Morgarath?" Maddie asked. She was unable to keep the skeptical tone out of her voice.

Glenys eyed her for several seconds, then nodded. "Aye," she said. "Morgarath."

"Morgarath isn't coming back," Will said firmly. "My friend Horace saw to that."

"That may be," Glenys admitted. "She had little success in that area. But she did find the direwolves. They were up in the mountains where Morgarath had his lair."

Will shook his head. "Lord knows what evil is up in those mountains," he said. "It's a wild, unexplored part of the world."

"True enough," said Glenys. "She found them and dominated them. Before long, they were raiding farms and taking animals."

Will turned to the two sons, who were watching their mother with wide eyes. "You saw one of these creatures," he said, and they looked at him and nodded. "Tell us about it."

"It stalked us," Gryff said. "We were finished work for the day and were heading home."

"Our field is two kilometers away," Glenys said.

Gryff nodded. "Just so. We were walking home together and we heard . . . something . . . in the rocks above us."

"Then we saw it," Dai said, taking up the tale. "It appeared in the rocks behind us. It was two or three times the size of a normal wolf. And it snarled at us." He shuddered at the memory. "It was a sound straight out of hell," he said.

"Then it made its way down to the track," Gryff put in, "and began moving toward us."

"Just a minute," Will said. "It actually began to attack you—three of you—in broad daylight?"

The two farmers nodded, their eyes wide with fear at the memory.

"It were late afternoon," Gryff amended. "But there was still plenty of light around. We backed up together as it came on—"

"You had weapons?" Maddie asked.

The two pairs of eyes turned to her. "We had our tools," Dai told her. "Rakes and hoes. But it didn't seem to be worried by them."

"It kept coming forward, snarling at us all the while. We stayed together for a few minutes, then we panicked and ran. Owen was the last to run. We were ahead of him."

"Owen was the slowest," Dai said sadly. "We heard the

wolf coming behind him, baying and howling. Then the sounds stopped."

"Did you see it take him?" Will asked, but the two farmers shook their heads.

"We knew what was happening," Gryff said. "There was no need for us to see it. We just ran for our lives." He dropped his head and wiped away a tear. "We left poor Owen to that creature," he said quietly.

Will moved toward him and laid a hand on his shoulder. "Don't blame yourself. There was nothing else you could do," he said.

Gryff looked up at him, his eyes tortured with guilt. "We could have helped him," he said in a small voice.

But Will shook his head. "You would have died with him," he told the miserable man. "That would have done him no good."

Gryff dropped his gaze and hung his head. Eventually, he replied. "Aye. I suppose you're right." When he appeared unable to continue, Dai took up the tale once more.

"We ran home and slammed the door behind us," he said.

"Did the creature follow you?" Maddie asked.

He thought about it, then shook his head. "No. It stayed with Owen. Least, I suppose so."

"They were terrified," Glenys said, remembering that dreadful evening. "Looked as though the hounds of hell were after them." She paused and shrugged. "As I suppose they were."

Gryff had recovered and resumed his account. "We could hear the creature howling through the night. We went out next morning with some of the men from the village and found poor Owen's body pretty much where we had left him. The wolf had torn him up badly and left him lying there." He shuddered at the memory. "We buried him that day and sent word to the nearest army post."

"Did they respond?" Will asked.

Gryff shook his head bitterly. "They did not. They sent word it must have been a wolf and there was little they could do about it. They have no hunters or trackers."

Will and Maddie looked at each other, then Will spoke. "Well, they sent word to Queen Madelydd, and she contacted King Duncan of Araluen. Madelydd wanted help finding and killing this beast. She asked for Rangers."

"We *are* hunters and trackers," Maddie put in.

Will nodded. "Just so. But we'll need as much information as you can give us about these wolves—and this woman, Arazan."

There was silence in the room for a few seconds, then Glenys spoke.

"Then you'll need to talk to Eveningstar," she said.

Once again, Maddie and Will exchanged a glance. Maddie frowned as she considered the name. "Eveningstar?" she said. "Who exactly is Eveningstar?"

"She's a good woman," said Dai, and Gryff nodded in silent agreement.

"Aye, she is that," Glenys agreed. "She lives farther up the mountain, on her own in a small cottage. And she knows about the dark side of nature."

"So, she's a witch?" Will asked. "A sorceress?"

Glenys paused as she considered the question. "Not exactly," she replied. "She's a healer. She understands herbs and potions. And she knows about spells and the black arts. For the past year or so, she's been trying to keep Arazan and her vile creatures in check."

"Without too much success, by the sound of it," Will said.

But Glenys shook her head emphatically. "Not so. On two occasions, when the direwolves have been raiding nearby villages, she's driven them off. She has certain powers."

"Is she as powerful as Arazan?" Maddie asked.

Glenys paused and thought again. "Possibly not," she said. "But she knows enough to keep herself hidden from the dark witch, and to protect herself against her."

"And you can tell us where to find this woman?" Will asked.

Glenys nodded. "We'll send you on your way in the morning. Better you stay here tonight. It's not safe out there in the dark hours."

"That suits me," said Maddie quickly, before Will could refuse the offer of hospitality. She had no wish to be wandering round these ill-favored mountains late at night. Will glanced at her and nodded agreement.

"Thanks for your hospitality," he said to Glenys. The elderly woman motioned to the pot simmering over the coals of the fire.

"We'll have supper first," she said, "then you can bed down by the fire."

"We ate at the tavern," Will said, but she made a dismissive gesture.

"Day-old bread and cheese! You want a good hot meal inside you on a night like this."

And as she said it, Will had to admit that the aroma coming from the rich vegetable stew in the pot made her argument a convincing one.

11

THE FLAGSTONES ON THE FLOOR WERE HARD AND UNYIELDING,
but at least they were even and without lumps. When Will and
Maddie spread their bedrolls under them in front of the fire
and covered themselves with their cloaks, they found the floor
made a relatively comfortable bed for the night. In addition, the
stones had absorbed the heat from the fire during the day, and
it radiated up underneath them as they lay down.

Gryff and Dai climbed the ladder into the loft at the far end
of the room and settled down there. Glenys retired to the back
room of the little house.

Maddie lay on her back, relishing the warmth of the stones
beneath her as she listened to Will's steady breathing. Outside,
the wind howled around the little house, making her glad they
were indoors and not camped among the rocks under a make-
shift shelter.

She thought over the events of the day and the information
they had gleaned from Glenys and her sons. She was cynical
about Glenys's belief in Arazan's dark powers. Maddie was not
superstitious, and she didn't hold with stories of ghosts and

ghouls or of people raising the dead. She made a mental note to ask Will about it the following day, when they were on the road. She wouldn't do it in front of Glenys and her boys, sensing that to do so would be an insult to them.

That Arazan had engaged with the direwolves was a matter for concern. But, as Will had said, the Mountains of Rain and Night held many secrets and throwbacks to an earlier time. It was possible that direwolves had survived up there, in spite of the fact that they hadn't been sighted in Araluen for hundreds of years.

Horrific as they might be, direwolves weren't supernatural creatures. They were flesh and blood and, as such, could be defeated by normal weapons. She smiled grimly to herself. Forbidding and savage as a direwolf might be, she couldn't see one standing up to the power of Will's massive longbow.

And with that comforting thought in her mind, she finally fell asleep.

They woke early the following morning. The wind had abated somewhat, although it was still brisk, and the clouds and rain had blown over during the night. The morning was bright and cold, and the villagers were up and about their day's work, heading off to their mines and farms, their tools over their shoulders. As Will and Maddie stood outside the little cottage, taking in the day, passersby eyed them curiously. Travelers were rare in Poddranyth, and judging by their clothing and weapons, the two Rangers were obviously not Celts.

Will offered some of their coffee to Glenys, and she brewed a large pot for the five of them, toasting the previous day's bread over the glowing coals of the fire and spreading it thickly with wild honey.

After they had breakfasted, Gryff and Dai fetched their tools from behind the house and prepared to set off for their field, bidding the Rangers farewell. They kissed their mother goodbye and she clung to them, all too aware that life in Celtica was perilous, remembering that only a few short weeks before, she had farewelled three sons one morning to see only two arrive back that night. But, direwolves or not, farm life was hard and unrelenting in Poddranyth. The fields had to be tended constantly and there was no respite, no time for slacking off.

"Take care," she told them. "Look out for each other."

"We will, Mam," Dai assured her, then, nodding farewell to the two Rangers, he and his brother strode off down the street, joining the growing crowd of people on their way to a day's work.

Will and Maddie packed up their bedrolls, and while Maddie went to saddle the horses, Glenys gave Will directions to Eveningstar's cottage.

"Follow the high street out of the village, alongside the gorge," she said, "opposite to the way you came in. After three-quarters of a kilometer, you'll see a flat-topped rock on the left side of the road. That marks the beginning of the path that winds up to Eveningstar's cottage. Follow it up the hill for five hundred meters and you'll come upon it."

"That sounds simple enough," Will said.

She eyed him speculatively. "It is that—so long as Eveningstar wants to be found," she told him. "She's been known to hide the way to her home in times past. She can conjure up a fog to confuse those she chooses not to see."

Will said nothing. It occurred to him that in these damp and rainy mountains, fogs might not be the result of any conjuring, but a natural occurrence. Still, out of respect for the woman, he didn't voice the thought.

Maddie arrived with the horses and Will moved to stand beside Tug, preparing to mount.

"Our thanks for your hospitality," he said. "And for the information you've given us."

"The hospitality was nothing," she said, adding with a slight smile. "You more than paid for it with that coffee of yours." She grew serious, looking at the two of them as Will swung up easily into the saddle. "Go safely," she said. "I know you're skeptical about Arazan and her powers, but take care nonetheless. Don't underestimate the dangers of the dark arts."

"We won't," he assured her. "And hopefully we can rid you of this problem."

He tapped Tug with his heel and they set off, heading back to the high street and turning left toward Eveningstar's cottage. Most of the mines and farms lay in the opposite direction, and they threaded their way through the stream of workers heading out for the day. Then they reached the outskirts of the little village and the traffic died away, leaving the road ahead empty. They had been riding in single file to allow the foot traffic room to pass. Now Maddie urged Bumper up alongside Tug. Will glanced at her, noting the frown of concentration on her face. He sensed what was coming.

"Something you want to ask?" he said.

"All this supernatural stuff—spells and the black arts and raising the dead—do you believe in it?"

A smile crossed Will's features, and he paused before

answering. "I once asked Halt the same question," he said, "when I was sent to investigate the sorcerer known as Malkallam."

"Malkallam?" she said. She'd heard the story. "But he wasn't a sorcerer, was he? He was using tricks to keep his people safe from harm. He became Malcolm the healer, didn't he?"

"He always was Malcolm the healer. Malkallam was a false identity he created to keep people out of Grimsdell Wood, where he had his compound."

"So sorcery *is* a fake?" she asked.

Again, he paused, selecting his words carefully. "Not quite. Here's what Halt told me. Ninety-five percent of what people believe to be magic and sorcery we can put down to lack of education, hysteria and superstitious fear. Three percent can be explained away as trickery and illusion. A further one percent is the result of mesmerism—hypnotism if you like—where people are convinced that what they are seeing is real, even though it's not."

He waited, letting her do the addition. Frowning, she spoke again.

"But that's ninety-nine percent. What about the other one percent?"

Will shrugged. "Exactly. That's what I asked him. And he told me there was no rational explanation for that remaining one percent. It remained a mystery."

"So-o-o," Maddie said, drawing out the word as she came to a conclusion. "You're saying Halt believes in black magic and sorcery?"

But Will shook his head. "Not quite. I'm saying he chooses not to *disbelieve* it. It may well be the reason behind that one percent of cases. After all, we know Morgarath had mental powers way out of the ordinary. And he used them to further his evil plans. He held control over the Wargals, using the power of his mind alone. Was that sorcery? Or was it something we just don't know enough about yet? Who's to say?"

Maddie shifted uncomfortably in her saddle. Her confident skepticism about witches and sorcerers and black magic was eroded by the realization that Will and Halt, two of the most well-informed and pragmatic people she knew, would not totally dismiss the idea that there were forces in the world beyond their knowledge or understanding.

"Somehow, I don't find that very reassuring," she said.

Will laughed softly. "Well, look at the numbers again. The odds are that this Arazan character is just a wicked old lady who uses tricks and illusions to make people afraid of her. There's only one chance in a hundred that she's really a sorceress."

"That's one more chance than I'm comfortable with," Maddie said. "But in any event, why would she want to make people afraid of her? What does she gain from it?"

"Think about it, Maddie. These hills are loaded with gold and silver. The Celts spend all their waking hours gouging it out of the rock. If she can enslave them or bend them to her will, she can make herself a very rich woman. Gold can make people do some pretty terrible things."

Maddie sighed unhappily. "That's true, I suppose," she said, but Will was pointing to a large flat rock on the left of the road.

"I'd say that's the turnoff to Eveningstar's cottage," he said. "Perhaps she can shed a little more light on the question for us."

They turned their horses off the main road and followed the narrow, winding track upward. After half a kilometer, they rounded a blind corner, where a large outcrop of boulders concealed the path ahead, and were confronted by a small, neat cottage. It was similar to the usual run of buildings in Celtica, but obviously maintained with greater care than the gray, drab stone houses they had seen so far. Its walls were freshly whitewashed, and there were flowers growing in tubs either side of the door, which had recently been painted a deep shade of green.

As they rode closer, the door opened and a petite woman with gray-streaked black hair and sparkling blue eyes emerged.

"Good morning," she said, smiling a welcome to them. "I've been expecting you. My name is Eveningstar."

12

As they dismounted, Maddie stepped close to Will.

"How did she know we were coming?" she whispered.

He shrugged and answered in the same lowered tone. "Maybe she had a message from Poddranyth."

The woman stood aside and ushered them into the cottage. The interior was much the same as Glenys's house, but brighter and more welcoming. There was a large rug on the floor, and three wooden armchairs were ranged around the fireplace. In addition, there were two large windows in the front wall on either side of the door. They were currently unshuttered and sunlight streamed into the room. A round table and four chairs formed the dining area, and the fireplace was once again the site for cooking.

A curtained doorway led off to the second room in the cottage—presumably Eveningstar's bedroom. Unlike at the ap-Jones house, there was no loft.

Eveningstar waved them to the armchairs and busied herself pouring water from a pottery jug into a blackened kettle, then swung it in over the fireplace to boil.

"Would you like tea?" she said.

Will hesitated. He would have preferred coffee, but it would seem graceless to say so. "That'd be fine," he replied.

"Just as well," she said cheerfully. "I don't have any coffee."

Will and Maddie exchanged a look. This bright-eyed woman seemed to know a lot about them. She smiled as she served them the hot mint tea in fine ceramic mugs. Will sipped his. He had to admit it was refreshing and invigorating—and nearly as good as coffee.

Eveningstar watched as they sampled the tea. She seemed gratified by their positive reactions, and took a sip of her own.

"I didn't get a message from Poddranyth," she said to Maddie. "I saw you coming."

"How?" Maddie asked. She glanced out the window. The solid rock bluff blocked the view of the road leading up to the cottage.

Eveningstar smiled at the question. "I didn't see you in that way," she explained. "I have the gift of farsight. I saw you in my mind."

"Oh," said Maddie. After her discussion with Will on the road up from the village, she was thrown off balance by Eveningstar's casual claim of mystic power. She looked to change the subject.

"Eveningstar. That's a very beautiful name," she said.

The woman nodded her head. "It's the result of a misunderstanding, actually," she said. "My name is Joan Evans-Stark. But when I first came here, people misheard it as Eveningstar, and that's what they started to call me. I decided I liked the name, so I didn't bother to correct them."

Maddie smiled at the woman. In spite of her casual reference to having farsight, there was something about her that was instantly likable—and trustworthy.

"I probably would have done the same," she said.

Will set his cup down, belatedly remembering his manners.

"My apologies," he said. "My name is Will Treaty, and this young lady is my apprentice, Maddie."

Eveningstar nodded in acknowledgment. "And you're Rangers, from Araluen," she said.

"That's right," Will replied. There wasn't anything mystical about her recognizing that fact, he thought. Plenty of people in Celtica knew about the Ranger Corps. He realized that Eveningstar was studying him closely, her head tilted to one side, rather like a bird.

"You've been here before," she said slowly. "In Celtica."

"Yes. But it was many years ago," he admitted. She frowned slightly, as if trying to remember something. Then her expression cleared.

"You're the one who burned the bridge," she said.

Will sat back, startled. For a moment, he was lost for words, and Eveningstar elaborated. "Morgarath's bridge, over the Fissure."

"That's right," he admitted. Then he recovered. It was possible that she knew his name. The tale of Morgarath's bridge had been often repeated over the years, although in those days he wasn't known as Will Treaty, simply as Will. But now Eveningstar was frowning at Maddie.

"And there's something about you too," she said thoughtfully, then dismissed the idea that was forming in her mind. "But you're too young. You couldn't have been here . . ."

There was a long, awkward pause, then Will spoke. "Maddie's mother was with me," he said.

Eveningstar nodded, as if her thoughts had all fallen into place. "Yes. That's it. I knew there was something about you."

"How?" Maddie asked, fascinated. "How did you know?"

Eveningstar shrugged. "I'm not sure. Sometimes I just sense

things about people. I sensed something about the two of you. Well, you're doubly welcome in that case. I'm delighted to have you in my home."

"Glenys Jones said you might be able to tell us more about the woman they call Arazan," Will said.

The smile faded from Eveningstar's face. "Yes. I'm not surprised your coming to Celtica has something to do with her," she said. "She's an evil, evil woman."

"We heard that she has a pack of direwolves who do her bidding," Will continued, and Eveningstar nodded.

"That's right. She discovered them on the plateau and gained control of them."

"They must have survived up there long after they became extinct in other parts of the country," Will said.

"Did you know she has also subjugated a band of Wargals?" Eveningstar asked.

The expression of shock on Will's face told her the answer. "Wargals? But they've been peaceful ever since Morgarath died!" he said. That old feeling of fear and loathing touched him, and he felt the hairs on the back of his neck stand up. As a boy, he had been terrified of Wargals; in his first encounter with them, he had frozen and it was only Halt's timely intervention that had saved his life. He shuddered at the memory.

Maddie regarded him uneasily. She was surprised to think that Will might be fearful of any creature.

Eveningstar nodded sadly. "Sad to say, she's managed it. She found one who was more advanced than the rest of the clan— Marko, she calls him. He has developed a higher level of intelligence. Apparently, he can even speak, although his vocabulary is limited, and his mouth and jaw aren't really suited to forming words. He helped her to gain control of a tribe of the creatures—about a dozen, all told."

Will shook his head. "All the more reason why we have to find her and stop her," he said.

"You know that she practices the black arts?" Eveningstar asked.

Will made a dismissive gesture. "I don't care how much abracadabra claptrap she spouts," he said. "But direwolves and Wargals are flesh and blood, and she can't be allowed to continue practicing that sort of evil."

Eveningstar leaned back in her chair and was silent for several seconds. Then she continued. "I'm not sure *claptrap* is a good description of what she does. There are forces in nature that we know very little about. But that doesn't mean they're not present—or that they're not powerful," she said.

Will snorted disdainfully. "Glenys said she was trying to contact Morgarath. To raise his spirit from the dead. I don't believe that's possible."

"I tend to go along with you there," Eveningstar agreed. "The dead are dead and have little or no power. But there are other forces—forces that are hidden from us. And they are incredibly powerful and incredibly dangerous. When she failed to bring Morgarath back, she began experimenting with those forces. I fear she's trying to raise a demon—to bring it across into this world."

Will said nothing, but he shook his head in disagreement. To him, demons, ghosts and goblins were all part of the same superstitious nonsense. They were the inventions of tricksters and charlatans.

Eveningstar read the expression on his face and sighed. "You do believe in evil, I take it?"

Will was reluctant to agree. "I believe there are evil people," he said. "I've seen plenty of them in my time."

"And you believe in good?" Eveningstar persisted.

Will immediately nodded. "Of course. There are plenty of people in this world who personify it."

"So, if there is a force for good, why shouldn't there be a force for evil?" she asked. "What made Morgarath so evil? What makes you so sure there is no evil force out there, driving the misdeeds of people like Morgarath—and Arazan?"

"Then show it to me," Will challenged.

She shook her head. "I can't," she said.

Will went to speak, but she hastened to talk over him. "But I can't show you good either. Oh, I can show you the manifestations of goodness, of honor and courage. But I can't show you the actual force of goodness. Yet it exists. So who's to say that evil doesn't exist? It may be outside of our sight, but it's there. There's a dark force that drives the evil in this world, and I tell you, people like Arazan tamper with it and try to use it to their own ends."

"So, you believe in demons?" Will asked.

She nodded emphatically. "Yes. I do. I believe they are a manifestation of evil. They exist outside our understanding and vision. But they're there. Arazan has made contact with one. She's courting it, if you like, cajoling it. Trying to force it to take physical shape. And tonight, I'll prove it to you."

13

Eveningstar left the two Rangers to their own devices for the rest of the day while she pottered in her garden, tending to her vegetable plot and the brightly colored flowers growing in tubs by the door.

Will and Maddie sat outside the house, enjoying the warm sun. They spoke little. Will was still somewhat taken aback by Eveningstar's having recognized him as the apprentice Ranger who had destroyed Morgarath's bridge and sensing Maddie's connection to her mother. Seeing his confusion, Maddie refrained from questioning him further about supernatural matters or the occult. They came to an unspoken understanding that they would see how matters transpired with this remarkable woman before making any more conclusions.

At noon, Eveningstar gave them crusty bread with sliced ham and cheese, and Will fetched their dwindling supply of coffee beans from his travel kit. Then, as the daylight began to fade and the sun's warmth left them, they went back into her cheerful little cottage and sat by the fire while she prepared supper for them—a hearty chicken hot pot with more of the bread, washed down by another pot of coffee.

Once the dinner plates were washed and put away, she began

to make preparations for the evening. Will and Maddie watched, fascinated, as she rolled back the rug, then drew a circle in chalk on the flagstone floor and placed three of the wooden dining chairs inside it. In the center of the chairs, she placed a brazier filled with glowing coals from the fireplace. Then she handed each of them a bunch of fresh rosemary on a long leather cord, which she instructed them to place around their necks.

"Rosemary confuses Arazan's farsight," she told them. "It will help conceal you from her. The chalk circle serves a similar purpose. This way, we can watch her without her being able to see us or know where we are."

"So she won't know we can see her?" Maddie asked.

Eveningstar pursed her lips thoughtfully before answering. "She may sense that someone is watching her," she replied. "And she'll assume it's me, as we've clashed on previous occasions. But she won't be able to see us or locate us." She paused, then added a warning. "Just be sure you don't speak or make any sound while we're watching her."

"What will happen if we do?" Maddie asked.

Eveningstar gave her an encouraging smile. "I'm not totally sure," she said. "I've never shown this to anyone before. It may expose you to her sight. But don't worry, she can't actually harm you as long as you're inside the circle."

Her words did little to reassure Maddie, who watched as the woman continued her preparations, hanging sprigs of rosemary around the room and grinding a green crystalline substance to a fine powder with a pestle and mortar. Maddie saw her lips moving as she did this and realized that Eveningstar was muttering an incantation of some kind.

Once it was fully dark, Eveningstar motioned for the two

Rangers to take their positions and, extinguishing the lamps in the room, she joined them. The only light sources now were the fireplace and the brazier full of glowing coals. The shutters were closed, keeping out the chill wind and the light from the rising half moon.

Eveningstar took her seat and pulled it closer to the brazier. "Ready?" she asked, and when they confirmed that they were, she added: "Make sure you have your rosemary. Watch the brazier. Watch the flames."

Maddie and Will both instinctively touched the bundles of the herb hanging around their necks and again replied in the affirmative. Their voices didn't rise above a whisper. Maddie's stomach was in a knot of tension, and her mouth was dry. She wished she'd thought to take a beaker of water inside the circle with her but sensed it was now too late to hold up proceedings. She became aware that her heart rate had accelerated considerably. She glanced at Will. He was leaning slightly forward, his eyes on the coals. The red light from the brazier reflected from his face. He looked tense and drawn.

"Watch the brazier," Eveningstar warned, seeing Maddie's sideways glance. Maddie quickly looked away from Will and peered intently into the bed of glowing coals. They pulsated, almost seeming to be alive, and her eyes began to water with the glow and the heat radiating from them.

She became aware that Eveningstar was chanting again, her voice seeming to come from a great distance as Maddie concentrated on the pulsing, glowing coals. She tried to make sense of the words but realized she couldn't understand them.

"*Ikab bledsr rimanatof,*" Eveningstar chanted softly. "*Ikab nimendir bledsr.*"

A stray breeze caught the burning coals and caused them to glow even more brightly. Maddie blinked, trying to clear her vision. The heat was becoming oppressive, she thought, in spite of it being a cold night.

"*Jako libindira ikab,*" the chant continued, then Eveningstar took a handful of the ground powder from the pestle and, reaching over the brazier, allowed it to trickle down onto the superheated coals.

There was a muted whoosh as the powder hit the flames, then a green smoke cloud formed above the coals. But there was something unusual about the cloud, and Maddie realized that it wasn't dispersing. It was hanging over the brazier, forming into a ball. She stared into it with aching, watering eyes as shapes began to appear inside the cloud. She blinked to clear away the tears and peered harder.

At first, the shapes were indistinct, but nonetheless terrifying for that. Initially, she saw the vague outline of a wolf's head—but it was like no wolf she had seen before. It was huge and the fur was unkempt. It snarled, revealing massive yellow fangs. Then it was supplanted by another image: a group of menacing creatures that walked upright, knuckles to the ground. They looked like a cross between a bear and a wolf, and they seemed to exude malevolence. Involuntarily, Maddie sat back in her chair.

And suddenly, the image changed and she could see clearly.

Inside the ball of green vapor, she could see a woman. She was short and heavyset, wearing a shapeless dark robe. The exact color wasn't clear because of the green tinge of the smoke, but Maddie guessed it was either purple or black.

Her face was round and fleshy, framed by short gray hair shaped in greasy, unkempt curls. Maddie guessed her age to be somewhere between sixty and seventy. She might have appeared benevolent and grandmotherly, except for two features. Her eyes were dark and forbidding, devoid of warmth or any hint of friendliness or compassion. And her mouth was downturned at the corners, so that she appeared constantly displeased with all that she surveyed.

Taken altogether, she was a grim figure, with a strong sense of menace about her. Maddie shivered. She was tempted to look at Will to see his reaction, but mindful of Eveningstar's instruction to remain looking into the smoke, she resisted the urge.

Arazan—for it was obviously she—appeared to be in a room similar to Eveningstar's parlor. She was kneeling on a stone floor in the center of a chalked five-pointed star, with a circle surrounding it, touching all five points. She rocked back and forth and her lips moved as she chanted an incantation. Maddie couldn't make out the words.

As Maddie watched, the sphere of green smoke shimmered, then settled once more. A second shape began to develop, outside the chalked circle.

It was difficult to define. It was more a sense that something, or someone, was there rather than a definite image. It faded in and out of focus, drawing the eye to it but never presenting a recognizable shape. At times, it would almost strengthen into a solid shape, then it would fade completely as the green vapor shimmered, only to begin forming once more a few seconds later.

For a moment, Maddie had a tantalizing sense that she could make out a pair of black, scaly wings surmounting a serpentlike body, then they too disappeared. Frustrated and fearful, she leaned forward to peer more intently. Yet the harder she stared,

the more the figure seemed to retreat into the vapor, losing defi-
nition and shape, sitting somewhere just beyond her conscious
vision so that she could sense its presence but not see it.

I'm trying too hard, she thought, and she made an effort to
relax and to unfocus her eyes on the vapor above the coals, seeking to sense the images there with her subconscious rather than
her physical senses. As she did, the image became clearer.

The serpent body was back, along with the scale-covered,
batlike wings. But now there was a head and a face to the body—
a face unlike any she had ever seen or imagined before. A face
out of a nightmare.

It was formed in hard planes and sharp angles, without any
softening curves or roundness to it. It was black-green, with
glowing, evil eyes and a fringe of broad, triangular spikes around
its neck. As she watched in horror, it opened its mouth to reveal
huge, blackened fangs set in multiple rows inside its jaw. A
forked tongue uncurled from inside the mouth and flickered in
the air, testing for foreign scents. Then the evil-looking thing
threw its head back and roared.

Maddie could hear no actual sound. Yet her subconscious
was aware of a deep, shattering noise. It was a manifestation of
utter evil, pulsating and echoing inside her brain, pinning her to
the chair. It froze her muscles so that—no matter how much she
wanted to move, to escape from this apparition—she was held,
unable to budge. And she knew that this would be the basis of
her nightmares for years to come.

Overcome by the horror of the apparition, she let out a
whimper of fear.

Instantly, the creature disappeared from sight, leaving only the image of the elderly woman inside her protective chalked barrier. Furious, Arazan looked up, seeming to stare directly into Maddie's horrified eyes.

"Who's there?" she demanded in a hoarse voice. And now Maddie realized she could hear her as the witch moved her head from side to side, trying to see through the green veil of smoke.

Maddie shrank back in fright. But Eveningstar's circle, and the bundle of herbs around her neck, seemed to defeat Arazan's attempt to penetrate the protective screen.

"That's you, isn't it, Eveningstar? Spying on me again, are you? I've warned you about this. One day I'll catch you unprepared and I'll be rid of your spying and snooping for good." Arazan's voice was cold with fury, then she hesitated as she appeared to sense something. "But there's someone else, isn't there? Someone is with you. Someone who . . ."

She paused and made a waving gesture with her hand, as if trying to disperse the cloud that obscured her vision. Maddie had a terrifying sense that she was suddenly uncovered, visible to the sorceress's eyes.

Immediately, Eveningstar clapped her hands. The sphere of green vapor imploded, collapsing in on itself with a sound like the rush of wings, and the vision was gone, leaving the three watchers seated around the red glowing coals of the brazier once more.

14

"PITY YOU SPOKE," EVENINGSTAR SAID TO MADDIE, WHO WAS breathing raggedly, her heart pounding, utterly shaken by the experience. "She nearly saw you there."

"Are you sure she didn't?" Maddie asked, her voice trembling. "I felt that she did . . . I felt that she could see me."

Will rose from his chair and moved toward her, putting his arm around her shoulders and comforting her.

"Are you all right?" he asked her.

She looked up into his calm, reassuring eyes and shook her head. "Did you see it?" she quavered. "Did you see it?"

He nodded grimly. "I saw it," he said, and they both looked to Eveningstar.

"What was it?" Maddie asked. "I've never felt such a sense of pure evil!" She shuddered at the memory, then asked anxiously, "Are you sure she didn't see me?"

Eveningstar shook her head. "She was beginning to penetrate the screen that protects me when I watch her. When you made a noise, that gave her something to fasten on to. But I broke the spell just in time. She may have caught a glimpse of you, but not enough to track you or find you again."

"What was that . . . thing?" Will asked, repeating Maddie's question.

Eveningstar met his gaze for a few seconds, then answered calmly. "That was a demon," she said. "Its name is Krakotomal. She's been trying to summon him for weeks but that's the closest she's come to bringing him across." She smiled grimly. "Maybe it's as well that you did make a noise," she told Maddie.

"What were the first images?" Maddie asked. "They were terrifying, but compared to the demon, they seem like nothing."

"The first creature was a direwolf," Eveningstar explained. "From what I've been able to determine, she has three of them. Then you saw some of the Wargals that Arazan has bent to her will. And I agree. They are horrific, but Krakotomal is pure evil." She looked up at Will. "Do you believe me now?"

He nodded sadly. "I'm afraid I do," he said. "How do you know so much about her?"

Eveningstar shrugged. "Arazan has been terrorizing the farmers and miners in this area for over three years. I've done my best to stop her, but she's very powerful. The best I can do is to limit her activities. But if she manages to summon Krakotomal . . ." She paused, letting the sentence hang.

"No word of this has ever reached Araluen," Will said.

"That's Celtica for you. A lot goes on down here that you never hear about in the north. But if she ever gains control of the demon, you'll hear plenty."

"She's planning to attack Araluen?" Maddie asked.

Eveningstar nodded. "She wants power, and real riches. And that means moving north from Celtica. With a demon to help her, no army will stand against her for long."

"We're going to have to stop her," said Will. "The question is, how?"

"There are ways to fight demons," Eveningstar told them. "I can help you with those."

Will met her gaze and they looked long and hard at each other for some time. "I think you're going to have to," he said finally.

Eveningstar nodded once and rose to her feet. "We'll talk more in the morning. But for now, it's been a long night. We should get some sleep."

"Sleep?" said Maddie, her voice rising in pitch. "How could you sleep after seeing that thing? I know I'll be awake all night!"

Eveningstar smiled at her. "I'll fix you a drink to settle your nerves," she said. "It'll help you to sleep. Then we'll talk tomorrow about how you can fight Arazan."

She poured milk into a small metal jug and moved it close to the coals of the fire to warm it. Then she mixed a selection of herbs in a pestle and mortar, grinding them to a fine powder. Finally, satisfied that the milk was warm enough, she tipped the powder into it and stirred, then poured it into a beaker and handed it to Maddie.

"Drink this," she said. "It'll take your mind off Arazan and her companions."

"I doubt that anything could do that," Maddie said. But she took the beaker and sipped it cautiously. From past experience, she knew that usually, when someone mixed herbs and told you to drink, the result was bitter and unpleasant. To her surprise, Eveningstar's drink was warm and sweet-tasting. She drank more deeply and drained the beaker, handing it back to Eveningstar.

"Thanks," she said. She could feel her rapid pulse slowing, her heart beating more regularly. After a minute or two, she yawned hugely and felt her eyelids growing heavier. To her surprise, the events of the night and the sights she had seen were becoming less distinct, fading into the background. She yawned again.

"Think I'll turn in," she said. She spread her bedroll on the floor by the fireplace and lay down, wrapping her cloak around her. Within minutes, she was breathing deeply. Will and Eveningstar watched her.

"Thanks for that," Will said, and the woman nodded.

"It was a lot for a young girl to witness," she said. "But she'll sleep through the night now." She regarded Will closely. "How about you?" she asked. "Are you all right, or will I mix you a draft as well?"

He shook his head. "I'll be fine," he told her. "I've seen my share of horrors in my time."

"If you're sure," she said, pausing to see if he'd change his mind. When he didn't, she continued. "We'll talk in the morning. There are some things you will need if you're going to confront Arazan."

"Oh, I'm going to confront her all right," Will said. "But perhaps I should leave Maddie here with you?"

To his surprise, she shook her head. "I think you'll need her help," she said. "The combination of Arazan, her demon, the wolves and the Wargals is a lot for one man to take on. And Maddie is stronger than you think. Not many people could have witnessed what she did without being terrified. I'll give you some more of the herbs I just gave her to help ease the memories. But she should go with you."

Will considered her words and nodded. He knew that Maddie was strong-willed and courageous. And she was a more-than-capable warrior with her sling and her bow. He realized he'd be glad of Maddie's support when it came to confronting the sorceress and her horrifying minions.

"You're right," he said. "I think I'll turn in as well. We'll talk in the morning."

"Get a good night's sleep," Eveningstar told him. She gestured toward the brazier full of glowing coals. "I might take another look in on Arazan during the night. If you hear noises, just ignore them."

"I'll do that," Will said. He spread his bedding out by the fire and settled down for the night. Eveningstar took the brazier and went into her small bedroom. After a few minutes, Will was conscious of a green-tinted glow showing around the edge of the curtain that covered the doorway. He shivered slightly at the thought of what Eveningstar might be seeing, then closed his eyes tight against the green light and allowed sleep to claim him.

Sunlight was streaming through the open shutters when he awoke. He glanced to one side. Maddie's bedding was rolled up. He could smell bacon, bread toasting and coffee brewing.

There are worse ways to wake up, he decided. He tossed his cloak aside and pulled on his boots. Eveningstar was busy by the fireplace, with bacon sizzling in an iron skillet and bread toasting on a rack over a pile of coals.

"Good morning," she said, then indicated the doorway. "There's a tub of rainwater outside if you want to freshen up. Maddie is tending to your horses."

"Thanks," said Will. He went outside and washed in the cold

water, shivering as he did so. Then he returned to the house, pulling on his shirt as he went. Eveningstar had laid out bread, bacon and coffee for him and he ate hungrily. She joined him, sipping a cup of herbal tea. She enjoyed coffee but she wasn't a fanatic like the Rangers.

"Did you see any more last night?" Will asked, through a mouthful of toast and bacon.

She shook her head. "Arazan seemed to have quit for the night," she told him. "I'm not surprised. It's exhausting work trying to raise a demon." She placed several sheets of parchment on the table between them, smoothing them down as she did so. "I prepared these for you," she said.

Will pulled them toward him and glanced at them. There was writing on them, but the words were in some foreign language that he didn't recognize.

"What are they?" he asked.

"They're incantations. You should learn them by heart. This one is a spell of banishment in case she does manage to bring Krakotomal across into this world. And this one is a shielding spell, to conceal you from Arazan's farsight. That way, she won't see you coming."

Will folded the sheets carefully and placed them inside his jacket.

"Thanks," he said. Prior to the events of the previous evening, he would have been skeptical about such matters. But, having witnessed Arazan's attempt to summon the demon, he was far more ready to believe in the value of incantations.

"And of course, don't forget to wear those bundles of rosemary," she told him. "They'll go a long way toward shielding you from her."

"Spells, incantations and bundles of herbs," he said. "Is there anything else we'll need?"

"Yes," she said. She rose and went to a chest of drawers set against the wall. She opened a small drawer at the top of the chest and took out a bundle wrapped in soft cloth. Returning to the table, she placed it in front of Will.

"You'll need to cast arrowheads with this," she said.

Setting down his coffee mug, he reached out for the small bundle. It was surprisingly heavy and emitted a metallic clinking sound as he picked it up. He unwrapped the cloth, which he saw now was chamois leather, and spilled the gleaming contents onto the tabletop.

"Silver," he said, as he recognized the small ingots contained in the parcel.

"That's right," she said. "Silver is a noble metal, and it has power against creatures from the occult." She paused meaningfully.

"Like Krakotomal?" Will said.

"Exactly. Ordinary weapons won't harm him. But weapons made from silver will be deadly to him. He can't stand them. The metal burns and scars his body—and penetrates the scales that cover him. That's why Arazan has subjugated the miners at Tenruath. She'll need a lot of silver to control Krakotomal, and the miners bring it to her. Her Wargals and the direwolves see to that."

Will arranged the half-dozen small ingots on the table. "This is worth a lot of money," he protested. "I can't take it from you."

Eveningstar shrugged. "What am I going to do with it?" she asked him. "I had the miners bring it to me because I was looking for a way to use it against Krakotomal. That's its only value to me, and I figure you're the best way to use it."

"I take it we don't need it against the direwolves and Wargals?" he asked.

She shook her head. "No. They're creatures of this world. Your normal iron arrowheads and blades will be fine against them." She paused. "Just make sure you hit what you aim at."

Will smiled grimly. "We usually do," he said.

15

THAT NIGHT, WILL AND MADDIE SAT CROSS-LEGGED BY A small fire they had built in the clear space in front of Eveningstar's cottage.

"The legends all say you should cast the arrowheads by the light of the moon," Eveningstar told them. "I'm not sure how much value to place on that, but it can't hurt to do it that way."

They placed a shovelful of coals from her fire into a hole they had dug in the ground, and Maddie tended to a small set of bellows, pumping steadily until the coals glowed red, then white, with heat. Then Will placed an iron crucible over the coals and placed two of the silver ingots into it. All this equipment came from his arrow-making kit, which he always carried with him.

Gradually, the silver ingots began to lose shape and liquefy under the intense heat from the coals. Smoke rose from the crucible and several impurities in the silver rose to the top of the glowing liquid. Will removed them with the end of a green stick, which sizzled and crackled as it touched the molten metal. Then he prepared his arrowhead mold, a hinged metal container with the shape of three arrowheads impressed in it. He smeared grease over the surface so that the arrowheads would slide out easily once the metal had cooled.

Maddie continued to pump at the bellows, keeping the heat high.

"Not too fast," Will cautioned her. "Keep it regular." She slowed to an easy, rhythmic pace.

Holding the long handle of the iron crucible in a cloth, Will tested the fluidity of the molten silver, swirling the pot and watching it slide around the crucible, smoking and glowing in the dim light.

Eveningstar, an interested spectator, peered over his shoulder. "That looks about right," she said.

Will grunted in reply, then flipped the mold closed, turning it on its side to expose the small hole through which he'd pour the molten silver.

It smoked and sizzled as he poured, continuing until a small amount of silver bubbled out of the aperture.

He set the mold down on the ground after tapping it gently against a large rock he had placed by the fire for that purpose. He glanced up at Eveningstar.

"That's to get rid of any bubbles or air pockets in the silver," he told her. "And now we wait."

He set the crucible down on the edge of the coals to keep the remaining metal molten. The mold smoked gently, gradually cooling down. As they waited, Will and Maddie took an arrow each and carefully slit the waxed cord that bound the iron arrowheads to the shafts. Once the binding was removed, they slid the arrowhead out of the deep notch cut in the top of the shaft. The arrowheads were triangular in shape, with a flattened tang extending from the base that fit tightly into the notch in the shaft. The edges of the blades were filed to a razor-sharp finish.

Maddie cut lengths of strong, thin cord to fasten the new arrowheads in place and put the lengths of cord into a small bowl of water. They would bind the heads to the shafts with the wet cord. As it dried, it would shrink and tighten.

Will tested the mold, touching it fleetingly with his finger. "Should be right by now," he said. He slipped the point of his saxe into the mold and levered it open. The three silver arrowheads glowed with heat and he lifted them out one at a time with a pair of pliers and plunged them into another bowl of water.

Steam hissed and billowed up as the heated silver touched the water. Will left the arrowheads to cool down further and moved the crucible back into the coals, motioning for Maddie to begin pumping the bellows once more. When he judged the molten metal was ready, he closed the mold and poured more silver into the aperture on the side. More steam and smoke rose around them as he did so. Again, he tapped the mold on a rock and set it aside to cool.

While he was doing so, Maddie began to bind one of the first three arrowheads into the notch at the front of the arrow. She wrapped the thin cord tightly around the wood, then tied it off. Once that was done, she smeared a quick-setting glue over the binding to make sure it didn't fray or work loose.

She held up the finished product for inspection, making sure the arrowhead aligned properly with the shaft, turning it this way and that. Will glanced at it and nodded approval.

"That looks good," he said. He nodded to a small file set among their tools. "You can start to put an edge on it now."

She began to rasp away with the file, grinding the side of the arrowhead to a sharp edge, then continuing the work with a whetstone. Will tipped the next three arrowheads into the bowl of water to cool and then selected one of the earlier warheads, binding it to an arrow shaft as Maddie had done.

Eveningstar noted that his actions were faster and more deft than Maddie's had been. "You've done this before," she commented.

He looked up and smiled. "Once or twice," he admitted. "But never before by the light of the moon."

An hour later, they had nine arrowheads set in their shafts and sharpened. Will took four and gave the remaining five to Maddie. He sat back, easing his stiff shoulders. He had been hunched over the fire and the mold the whole time.

"Let's get some sleep," he said, and tossed dirt over the fire to quench it.

Maddie rose, placing her five new arrows into her quiver, keeping them in a separate section she had fashioned.

"Did you want another sleeping draft?" Eveningstar asked, but Maddie shook her head and smiled. The activity of making arrows had restored her spirits to a great degree. The knowledge that she possessed a weapon that would kill the demon boosted her confidence.

"I'm all right now," she said.

She and Will packed up their arrow-making tools and went inside, settling down by the fire once more.

This time, Maddie slept easily through the night.

"Tenruath is only ten kilometers from here as the crow flies," Eveningstar told them next morning as they prepared to leave.

"But you'll have to backtrack along the gorge to the bridge where you crossed at Poddranyth, then swing north again on the other side."

Will checked his map and saw that she was right. "There are no other villages between here and Tenruath?"

She shook her head. "Unfortunately, no. You'll be camping out tonight. You should reach Tenruath around noon tomorrow. The high street runs uphill through the village. Arazan's house is the second-to-last on the left-hand side, at the top of the hill. It's the largest house in the village."

Will snorted disdainfully. "That comes as no surprise," he said.

Eveningstar nodded. "She'll know you're in the area, and she'll have her creatures looking for you. I'd advise you to keep a good watch tonight."

Will nodded. "We'll do that," he said. He swung up onto Tug's back. Maddie was already mounted. Bumper was fidgeting, eager to be on their way.

"Thanks for all your help," Will told the slightly built woman.

Eveningstar inclined her head. "It's little enough, but it should see you safe. At least now you know what you're heading for." She looked at Maddie. "How are you? Have you got the herbs for that sleeping draft?"

Maddie patted the satchel that she wore slung over one shoulder. "In here," she said. "But I think I'm fine now. I doubt that I'll need them."

"Don't be too sure," Eveningstar told her. "The mind can be a strange thing. Everything may seem fine here in the morning sunlight, but when you're camped out among the rocks in the dark, things can look a little different. And don't be reluctant to use them if you need to. There's no shame in accepting whatever help you can get."

Maddie smiled her thanks for the advice. "Thanks, Eveningstar. I'll keep that in mind."

Will raised his hand in farewell. "Once again, thanks for your help. We'll be on our way."

"Take care. If you need to contact me, sit down in a quiet place just before sunset and clear your mind of all distractions. I'll be looking for you then. But don't do it unless you have to. If we're making contact, she might be able to sense us." Eveningstar raised her own hand in an informal gesture of blessing. "And look after your girl."

Maddie grinned. "Bumper does that for me," she said. The little horse pricked up his ears as she said his name. Then the two Rangers wheeled their horses and trotted away from the neat little cottage, heading for the road back to Poddranyth. As they reached the rock outcrop that marked the turn onto the down-hill path, Maddie glanced back at the house.

But, in spite of the bright midmorning sunshine, a swirling white ground mist had arisen, concealing Eveningstar's cottage from view.

"That's strange," Maddie said.

Will, seeing the direction of her gaze, looked back as well. "There's a lot that's strange about this place," he said, recalling Glenys's words when she had directed them to the cottage: *so long as Eveningstar wants to be found.*

"I feel better knowing that she's on our side," Maddie said.

Will nodded agreement. "We're certainly better equipped than we were before we met her," he replied.

Maddie regarded him curiously. "Does it feel weird, Will?"

she asked. "After all, this whole affair seems to go directly against what you believed."

He didn't answer for several seconds. The events at Eveningstar's cabin had shaken him, forcing him to reassess long-held beliefs. His mind went back to an earlier time, when he was riding through the night to find help for a mortally ill Halt, and had sensed an unnatural presence on the site of an ancient burial field.

"Let's just say this is part of that one percent we don't know about," he answered eventually.

16

There were a few people abroad in Poddranyth as they rode through. Most of the villagers were at work in the fields or the mines nearby. Those who weren't looked up fearfully at the two cloaked figures. Word of their arrival, and their subsequent departure in search of Eveningstar, had spread rapidly through the village in the past few days. It didn't take long for the villagers to put two and two together and surmise that the Rangers were planning to confront Arazan and her direwolves. As a result, the Celts avoided making contact with them. Several women were seen to make the warding sign against evil in their direction.

They had all learned by bitter experience that it was unwise to become involved with anyone who opposed the sorceress of Tenruath.

Will and Maddie left Poddranyth behind them and turned onto the stone bridge across the ravine.

"Friendly lot," Maddie said, jerking her head back at the village.

Will shrugged. "Can't blame them for keeping their distance."

As Eveningstar had told them, once across the bridge they had to turn back north for Tenruath. They rode on through the day, stopping after noon to rest and water the horses, and brewing a pot of coffee to wash down their simple meal of bread, dried meat and fruit. The afternoon wore on, and as their shadows lengthened, they began to look for a place to make camp for the night.

They found a small clearing, sheltered on all sides by the rocks and well hidden from the road. A narrow gap among the boulders gave access to the clearing, which was roughly circular in shape and had an even, sandy floor. A nearby spring sent fresh, clean water cascading across the rock. They filled their canteens and a leather bucket for Tug and Bumper, then unsaddled the horses, rubbing them down with their saddle blankets, which they spread out on the rocks to air.

"I take it we're not lighting a fire?" Maddie said.

Will, mindful of Eveningstar's warning, shook his head. "Might be a little risky. We don't know where Arazan's wolves might be prowling and a fire would give us away."

They ate another cold meal, washed down with water. Maddie looked around the little clearing. A fireless camp was a cheerless way to spend the night, she thought. But she recognized the thinking behind it. The smell of woodsmoke would be noticeable for kilometers in the cold, clear air—particularly to creatures like direwolves, which, if they were like normal wolves, would have a keen sense of smell. And the glow of even a small fire would be all too obvious. At least, she thought, it wasn't raining.

"I'll take the first watch," Will said, and she laid out her bedroll and wrapped her cloak around her. It was full dark now, and without a fire there was little to do in the camp except rest. But she was tired after a day in the saddle, so she settled down to sleep.

She lay awake for a long while, listening to the sounds of the night. Somewhere in the distance, an owl hooted repeatedly, and there were scurrying sounds and rustling in the rocks as small animals or insects moved about. In spite of her glib reassurance to Eveningstar that she had regained her confidence after the night when they had observed Arazan, she realized there was a difference between being behind the cottage's stout stone walls and barred door and lying out here among the rocks, under the stars, where every unidentified sound could herald the presence of a direwolf stalking them.

The sound of the two horses as they moved about the campsite gave her some reassurance. If there was danger close by, Bumper and Tug would sound a warning. She turned over restlessly, touched her hand to the hilt of her saxe lying beside her head, and closed her eyes.

Something woke her—a sound different from the other sounds of the night she had grown accustomed to. Maddie lay still, keeping her breathing regular, and listened again for whatever it had been.

The owl was silent now, and the insects and lizards and small nocturnal animals were no longer skittering among the rocks. Moving her eyes only, she swiveled her gaze to where Will sat, his back against a large boulder, his bow across his knees.

His head was slumped forward, his face hidden in the shadows of his cowl.

She heard the noise again. It was a faint scrunching sound

of coarse sand and small pebbles being crushed underfoot by someone—or something—moving among the rocks.

Will didn't move and she realized with shock that he had fallen asleep—an almost unheard-of lapse on his part. Her heart beat faster as she fought down a wave of panic.

She wondered why the horses hadn't sounded a warning. Normally, their keen senses would pick up any stranger approaching the camp. But they were silent.

Scrunch . . . scrunch . . .

The noise was coming closer. Maddie sensed it was coming from the direction of the narrow gap in the rocks that led to the road. Something was moving toward her. Her mouth was dry and she could hear the blood pounding in her ears. Moving with infinite caution, she turned slowly, a centimeter at a time, until she could face the gap in the rocks. She peered through slitted eyes and made out a dark, shaggy shape in the shadows. There was no sign of the horses.

Scrunch . . . scrunch . . .

The shape padded forward, moving on all fours. As it came out of the narrow gap, it emerged into the moonlight.

Her throat constricted in terror as she recognized the evil form of a direwolf, only meters away. She opened her mouth to call a warning, to rouse Will, but no sound came.

The creature padded forward another pace. She lay rigid, unable to speak or move, frozen with terror. She had changed her position while she was asleep and her saxe was half a meter away from her hand. Try as she might, she couldn't move now to seize it.

Scrunch . . . scrunch . . .

Slowly, inexorably, the creature moved closer. Its yellow eyes glowed in the moonlight as it fixed its gaze on her. In another few paces, it would be upon her. Yet still she lay frozen, incapable of moving, as the direwolf approached.

Then it opened its massive jaws in a terrifying, silent snarl. She could see the rows of gleaming fangs set in the powerful jaws—jaws that could crush bones and rend flesh. Now it was barely a meter away and she could smell its rank breath and still her limbs were paralyzed with terror.

She tried to scream, but all that she could manage was a small, mewling whimper. And now the direwolf was reaching out one of its forepaws and touching it to her shoulder . . .

"Are you all right?" Will said, from close beside her. Her eyes snapped open and she was awake. He shook her shoulder gently once more, and she glanced around, panic-stricken, searching for the wolf.

But there was no sign of it and she realized, as the terror subsided, that she had been dreaming. There was no wolf. Will wasn't asleep on watch, and the two horses were close by. As she lay there, limp and terrified, Bumper moved closer to her and leaned down, letting his warm breath touch her face, sensing that all was not well with her.

"I was dreaming . . ." she said in a weak voice. "I was dreaming and I saw a wolf and I couldn't move . . . or speak . . . and you were asleep and the horses weren't here . . . and I . . ."

Bumper shook his head and rattled his mane. *Of course I was here,* she heard in her mind. *You know I'd never desert you.*

She reached out her hand and stroked his soft muzzle.

"I know . . ." she said weakly. Then she stopped. She had never told Will that her horse spoke to her in her mind, or that she answered him.

Will looked away. He understood and he realized it was a private matter for her—one she didn't want to discuss. Then he patted her shoulder again.

"It's all right," he told her. "There's no wolf. You were having a nightmare—and I don't wonder, with all you've seen in the past few days."

She sat up, wriggling her back against the boulder behind her and wiping a hand across her face. She realized her skin was damp with perspiration.

"I've got some of the herbs that Eveningstar gave us," he said. "Do you want me to mix them up in a sleeping draft?"

She shook her head. "I'm okay now. It just all seemed so real . . ." Her voice trailed away and she shook herself, tying to dispel the paralyzing fear she had felt as the direwolf closed in on her. She looked up at the moon and saw that it had moved through a giant arc while she had been asleep. "How long have I been asleep?" she asked.

Will shrugged. "A little over three hours. It's almost time for your watch."

He sensed that she would be better off having something positive to do rather than trying to get back to sleep. She tossed aside her cloak and stood, buckling on her belt with the double scabbard. The weight of her saxe and her throwing knife on her hip was a comforting sensation. She strung her bow and hooked her quiver onto her belt, then donned her cloak once more.

"You get some rest," she told Will.

He looked at her carefully. "You're sure you're all right?"

She nodded. "I'll be fine. I couldn't get back to sleep now anyway."

She paced around the little clearing, calming her nerves while

Will settled down to sleep. Then she found an outcrop of rock facing the gap in the boulders and settled down on it. It was uneven and it dug into her thighs uncomfortably, but that was all to the good. It would prevent her falling asleep on watch, she thought. Then she smiled grimly to herself.

Not that there's much chance of that, she thought.

17

An hour before dawn, Maddie roused Will to take the watch again.

As was his custom, he woke instantly as she laid a hand on his shoulder, but lay still for several seconds, assessing the situation, searching for any signs or sounds of danger. Then, satisfied that there was nothing to fear, he sat up and pushed his cloak aside.

"Everything all right?" he asked Maddie.

She smiled wanly. "Everything's fine. No direwolves in sight or sound—unless you dreamed about them."

He strung his bow and took his place on the rocks while she rolled back into her cloak and settled down. The three uneventful hours perched on the uncomfortable rock had eased her mind a great deal. And now she was really tired. She fell quickly into a deep and untroubled sleep.

It was full light when she awoke. Will was busy building a small fire with dry, clean-burning twigs.

"I think we can risk a fire now," he said. "The horses are showing no sign of anything in the near vicinity. And if there is a wolf around, it'd be able to see us anyway." He paused, then added, "More importantly, we'll be able to see it."

She nodded gratefully. The thought of a cup of honey-sweetened coffee was a welcome one. A few minutes later, she sat hunched over the small fire, a hot mug of coffee held between her cold hands. She sipped at the fragrant brew, feeling its warmth run through her like liquid fire. Will handed her a piece of flatbread and a slice of smoked venison. She chewed the tough meat, letting her saliva soften it as it formed savory juices.

"So, what do we do today?" she asked.

Will chewed his own piece of jerked meat, then replied. "We head for Tenruath and see what Arazan has in mind. We've half a day's ride, so there's no hurry."

The sun was fully risen by the time they got going, although its rays didn't reach into the circle among the rocks where they had camped. As they rode back onto the main road once more, they could feel its warmth against them.

It was another bright, clear day, and they rode on through the morning without incident. Around the eleventh hour, the terrain changed. The road, which had previously been bounded by a rock wall on one side and a steep drop on the other, veered away from the chasm and led them through a steep defile, lined either side by high rock faces.

Will reined in Tug as he approached the narrow passage and eyed it warily. Maddie, who had been riding behind him, eased Bumper up beside Tug.

"Problem?" she asked.

He gestured toward the narrow, rock-bound track that lay ahead of them. "That's a good place for an ambush," he said. "I don't like the look of it."

Maddie studied the narrow path through the rocks. "There doesn't seem to be a way round it," she pointed out.

Will nodded. "That's what I don't like. It's the only way through." He stood in his stirrups and looked around on all sides. Then he sat back and took an arrow from his quiver, nocking it to the bowstring. "Nothing for it but to go through," he said. "Keep an arrow nocked and your eyes and ears open."

He rode forward into the narrow gully. Maddie followed a few meters behind him, twisting continually in the saddle to check the rear.

They had gone about fifty meters when he held up a hand in warning. She brought Bumper to a halt, then eased up beside Will once more on the narrow track. Bumper rumbled a low warning deep in his chest. Tug responded in kind.

"Something's tracking us," he said softly, and gestured toward the top of the rock wall on their left. "We'll go forward six paces, then stop and listen."

Understanding what he had in mind, she pushed her cowl back clear of her head and touched Bumper with her heel. Together the two shaggy horses moved forward. After they had gone six paces, both riders checked them.

He heard a faint scraping sound from above and behind them—the sound of a clawed foot scraping on rock as its owner hurried to stop in time with them. Again, the horses rumbled a warning. Will patted Tug's neck.

"Easy, boy," he told the little horse. "We hear you."

Satisfied that his warning had been received, Tug stopped the low rumble in his chest. Bumper did the same. But both horses had their ears pricked, and they moved with a light-footed step, ready for danger.

Will pushed back his own cowl and angled his head to listen more carefully.

"It's moving past us," he said in the same soft tones. Maddie could just hear the sounds of something moving on top of the rocks to their left.

"Don't look," Will cautioned her. He nodded his head to a spot ahead of them, where the gully widened slightly. "That's the danger point," he said, and Maddie nodded in agreement. The direwolf, if that was what it was, would have more room to launch an attack there. Instinctively, she drew back the arrow some ten centimeters, then let it down again. There was no point in holding the bow tensed; she could draw back and shoot in a matter of seconds if it became necessary. Will heard the creak of her bow as she released the tension and nodded approvingly.

"Good," he said.

Then, seconds before they expected it, the attack came.

A huge shape appeared at the top of the rock wall to their left and launched itself at Will, snarling and snapping as it came. Bumper neighed in warning. Maddie brought her bow up to shoot but was hampered by being in the saddle—a less-than-ideal position for accurate shooting.

The direwolf, veteran of many such attacks, was acting instinctively. It knew that nine out of ten animals would panic at its sudden appearance and react by shying away from it. So it calculated its leap accordingly.

But Tug was a combat-trained Ranger horse. He had carried Will successfully through dozens of battles, and he'd been aware of the wolf's presence for some minutes. Accordingly, he didn't react as the majority of horses would have. Instead, he swerved and bounded sideways *toward* the attacker, moving under its leap and throwing off the attack.

The wolf struggled, twisting in midair to change the trajectory of its leap, but it was already committed. It soared over the horse and rider, failing to make the direct, crashing contact it had planned. Its jaws, ready to tear Will's throat and upper body, snapped harmlessly at empty space.

But it did make contact. Its hindquarters hit Will in passing—a glancing blow, but enough to throw him off balance.

That, coupled with his fighting to adjust to Tug's sudden, violent sideways leap, was enough to unhorse him. He felt himself falling and kicked his feet clear of the stirrups, landing heavily on the sand-and-rock floor of the gully.

The wolf landed several meters away, skidding on the sand and crashing onto its side, its eyes flaring with rage, its massive jaws snapping and snarling. Unhurt but infuriated, it sprang to its feet, twisting to face toward its quarry—the green-and-gray-cloaked figure slowly rising to its hands and knees.

That was its second mistake.

In its long life, the wolf had never known another animal to stand and fight. The inevitable result of an attack like this was for the quarry to panic and flee. But now the stocky gray horse was dancing toward it, light-footed and agile. As Will rose to his feet, Tug danced in at the crouching wolf, which was surprised by this unexpected show of aggression.

Maddie, seeing Will sprawl on the ground, had slipped from Bumper's saddle, drawing back the arrow she had nocked. But Tug was in her line of sight, blocking any shot at the wolf. And Bumper was prancing forward to join his friend.

"Tug!" Will shouted, terrified that his horse would be caught by those great snapping jaws. "Get away!"

But Tug ignored the command, dancing sideways, cutting back from side to side to keep the wolf confused. Then, in a flash, he pirouetted on his front hooves, putting his head down and raising his hind legs off the ground. In one smooth movement, he swung around and delivered a thundering kick with his hind legs—a kick that had all the strength and power of his muscular hindquarters behind it.

His ironshod hooves crashed into the wolf's side, cracking three ribs and hurling the huge animal across the clearing to smash into the rough rock wall behind it.

The wolf howled in rage and agony as it thudded sideways into the hard rocks.

Its left rear hip was dislocated by the violent impact, and it struggled to rise, only to slide back down to the sandy floor of the gully. And now it learned another lesson as Bumper danced forward on his hind legs, his forelegs flailing and striking at the wolf's head in a bewildering, rapid fusillade of hammer blows.

Just as the wolf had never known another animal to stand and fight against it, it had never before seen two animals combine in an attack like this. Confused, it tried to back away, but the rocks behind it held it fast. And for the first time in its life, the wolf felt fear.

Like Tug, Bumper was shod with iron horseshoes, which smashed into the wolf's muzzle, lacerating the skin and breaking bone beneath it.

Maddie watched, fearing for her horse. But Bumper was unrelenting. The wolf tried to snap at him, but the speed of Bumper's attack, and the fact that the wolf was unable to move freely, defeated the savage animal. Bloodied and battered, it fell back, and as Bumper finally retreated, it snarled its hatred at the two horses.

Will's arrow, powered by his eighty-pound longbow and at a range of just over four meters, struck straight into the snarling mouth and emerged through the base of its skull, severing the wolf's spine.

And the wolf fell dead on the sand.

18

WITH AN ARROW NOCKED READY ON HER BOWSTRING, MAD-
DIE MOVED TOWARD THE WOLF TO STUDY IT MORE CLOSELY.
She was ready to shoot in a heartbeat if the beast showed any
sign of life, but there was no need. It was well and truly dead.

She shook her head in wonder. "I can't believe our horses did
this," she said quietly. "I was terrified they'd be bitten."

"Tug hates wolves," Will said. "My first Tug was savaged by
a wolf and had to be retired."

Maddie looked up at him. "But that would have been years
ago. How does this Tug know about it?"

Will shrugged. "If it's in my mind, he knows," he said simply.

Maddie pursed her lips in surprise. This was the first time
that Will had ever intimated that he was in mental contact with
his horse, and she realized what she had long suspected, that the
bond she had with Bumper wasn't unique.

She set her bow down and unfastened the satchel hanging
round her neck, taking out paper and a charcoal pencil.

"What are you doing?" Will asked as she began to sketch the
dead monster.

"George asked me to bring him updated details of any dire-wolf we encountered," she told him. "There are a few things that aren't quite accurate in his reference piece."

Will smiled at the memory of his old wardmate. "Good old George," he said. "He's a stickler for detail." He angled his head for a closer view of Maddie's work as she quickly sketched the dead wolf. She was a good artist, he saw, and the likeness was an accurate one. When she had finished, he helped her lay out the wolf's body and measure it from nose to tail and then from shoulder to paw. She noted the measurements on her sheet and then folded it and put her materials away. Then, leaving the body for the crows and carrion eaters, they mounted and set out for Tenruath.

The road soon veered out of the confines of the gully and resumed its course along the side of the deep ravine—with the precipitous drop on their left and the steep rock walls on their right.

"Stay alert, boys," Will told the horses, leaning forward to pat Tug on the neck. The little horse responded with a snort and rattled his mane indignantly, as if to say, *There's no need to tell me that. I'm always alert.*

Maddie rode a few paces behind Will, constantly twisting in the saddle to check their back trail. But there was no further sign of any of Arazan's beasts. The road was empty of traffic.

They passed the time without speaking, the silence broken only by the steady clopping of their horses' hooves and the occasional clash of an iron horseshoe on rock. After several hours, the road veered away from the precipice again and ran through scrubby fields planted with crops. Occasionally, they could see mine shafts, marked by windlasses above them. They saw no sign of any local inhabitants.

Eventually, the road started to slope uphill, and finally, they came in sight of the village of Tenruath.

They brought their horses to a halt to study the village. They could see several people moving between the buildings, although so far the Rangers had gone unnoticed.

The houses themselves were built in the usual Celtic style—stone walls with low overhanging eaves and roofed with split-stone tiles. The houses were in various states of repair. Some had been whitewashed recently. Others were patchy and marked, the paint blistered and stripped by the driving wind and rains that were so frequent in this high country.

There was a common grazing ground at the start of the village, and they dismounted and left the horses there. Will gestured for Maddie to take one side of the road, and he took the other. Together, they moved into the village, staying close to the houses, arrows nocked to their bows and all senses alert.

They could see Arazan's house clearly. As Eveningstar had told them, it was the largest in the village and was set almost at the top of the hill.

"So, what's the plan?" Maddie asked.

Will chewed his lip thoughtfully. "We'll go in on foot," he said. "Stay close to the houses. Have your bow ready, and if anyone—or anything—tries to stop us, don't hesitate to shoot."

"You mean like a direwolf?" Maddie asked, noting his use of the word *anything*.

"Exactly. Or a Wargal."

"What about Arazan herself?" Maddie asked.

"We'll try to take her prisoner. When we get to her house,

we kick the door open and charge in. With any luck we'll take her by surprise, and we should be able to overpower her."

"Unless she has her pet demon with her," Maddie said.

Will hesitated. "Eveningstar said she hasn't actually raised him yet. But have one of your silver-headed arrows ready, just in case."

Maddie pursed her lips doubtfully.

Will noticed her expression. "What?" he said.

"Kick down the door and charge in," she said. "It's not the most complicated plan, is it?"

"Simple is good. The simpler it is, the less that can go wrong," Will replied.

"So you say," she said. But when she thought about it, she couldn't come up with a better alternative.

"Let's get moving," Will said.

Maddie's nerves hummed like a taut string as she crept slowly up the hill. So far, their arrival had gone unnoticed by the few people moving about the village. But that could change at any time.

Suddenly, the door of the house she was passing flew open and a middle-aged woman stepped out, a shopping basket slung over her arm. She halted in shock at the sight of the cloaked, armed figure moving past her home. She opened her mouth to cry out, but Maddie forestalled her.

"Stay quiet!" she snapped.

The woman closed her mouth, her eyes fixed on the gleaming warhead of the arrow nocked to Maddie's bowstring. Maddie gestured with the arrowhead, pointing it toward the half-open door behind the woman.

"Get back inside," she ordered, and after a startled second or two, the woman complied, the door slamming shut behind her. Maddie heard a soft whistle from across the road and glanced at Will. He was watching her, his eyebrows raised in a question. She signaled that all was well, and they resumed their uphill path.

Now the few villagers in the street began to notice the two stealthy figures moving up the hill. They stopped and stared, then hurried to their respective houses and went inside, closing the doors firmly behind them. Within a short time, the street was deserted. Maddie continued to scan the shadows between the houses, checking constantly behind them to make sure there was no enemy creeping up on them. But there was no sign of anyone. An expectant silence hung over the village like a pall.

She was conscious of eyes upon them and she realized that they were being watched from behind the windows of dozens of the small houses. A dog began barking suddenly as she passed close to one cottage, and she jumped in shock at the sudden noise. But a voice from inside the house scolded the dog, and it fell silent once more.

She was two doors away from Arazan's house when Will's soft whistle sounded again. She glanced quickly at him and he indicated for her to wait and that he was coming to join her. She stopped by the end of the house she was passing and he slipped quickly across the road, moving smoothly and silently to stand beside her. She gave him a questioning look.

"It all looks very quiet," he said softly.

She nodded. "I was thinking the same thing. Maybe she's not here."

"Or maybe she is and she's waiting for us to walk into a trap," he said.

She felt her heart beating faster as he said it. She'd been hoping he'd agree with her assessment of the situation. "So what do we do?" she asked.

He grinned at her. "Walk into the trap, I suppose."

He gestured toward Arazan's house, a few meters away. "Let's move up to the door. On my signal, you kick it open and I'll barge in."

She took a deep breath, then nodded. "All right. Let's get kicking and barging."

"Stay below the windows," Will cautioned her, and they started forward. There were three windows facing onto the street. As was the custom, they were covered in scraped, translucent oilskin. The two Rangers stooped as they came to each one, crouching low as they passed, then standing erect once more. The oilskin wasn't transparent, but their shadows would show all too clearly to anyone inside the house.

They moved silently, testing the ground beneath their soft boots with each pace, avoiding anything that might make a noise. It was a skill the Rangers had perfected and practiced over the years.

Will stopped as he reached the door. He looked at the base and saw there was a gap of several centimeters between the ground and the bottom of the door. He stepped away from the house, knowing that his shadow would be visible under the door if he stayed close by the wall. When he was past the door, he moved back in against the wall, then paused to listen.

Silence. No sound came from the house.

He leaned closer to the door, ears alert for any sound of movement. But there was nothing, just the soft sound of the ever-present wind stirring the dust in the high street. He looked at Maddie, a question in his eyes, but she shook her head. She could hear nothing either. The seconds dragged on but the house seemed deserted.

Still he waited, loath to go through that door and confront whatever might be awaiting him there. He knew that Arazan had recruited a band of Wargals. There could be half a dozen of them waiting inside the door in the darkened house. The old fear came back to him as he remembered his first encounter with the horrific beasts, so many years ago. Then he shook his head. Wargals couldn't remain absolutely silent for any length of time. He would have heard them grunting or shuffling their feet on the packed earth floor if they were there. Wargals were savage and pitiless, but they weren't stealthy.

On the other hand, wolves *were* stealthy, and there were still two of the direwolves unaccounted for. He took a deep breath, conscious that Maddie was watching him, waiting for his signal. He looked at her now and saw no sign of impatience, and he realized she understood his reluctance to challenge the unknown dangers behind the door. She nodded encouragingly at him and he came to a decision, pointing to the door and nodding.

He crouched, ready to leap through the door, an arrow nocked and half drawn on his massive bow.

Maddie stepped away from the house, got her balance, then sprang off the ground, straightening her right leg and smashing a flat-footed kick at the warped timbers of the door, close to the point where the latch was secured into the door frame.

The timber and plaster holding the latch was old and rotten

and crumbling. The force of Maddie's kick smashed the latch clear out of the door frame and sent the door flying open.

A fraction of a second later, Will hurled himself through the open door, bow raised and ready, spinning quickly to cover the room inside, the arrow now fully drawn and ready to shoot.

The room was empty.

19

THERE WAS A DOORWAY LEADING TO THE BACK ROOM OF THE house. It was covered by a heavy curtain. He moved silently toward it now, arrow half-drawn, bow raised, and jerked it to one side, springing forward into the second, smaller room.

It was sparsely furnished, with a bed, a small table and a chair. A half-burned, unlit candle was set on the bedside table. There was a rail set into the rear wall, presumably for hanging clothes. But it was empty.

Will moved back to the larger main room of the house and called softly to Maddie. "Nobody home. Come on in."

She entered, replacing the arrow she had kept nocked in her quiver. Her right hand stayed close to the hilt of her saxe as she moved farther into the room. Will was busy opening the three windows, letting sunlight in. The heavy shutters on the inner side of the windows were already drawn back and fastened to the wall.

There was no sign of anyone living in the house. The ashes of the fire were cold and the few pots were hanging on hooks beside the fireplace. There was a table with four stools set around it. In one corner, a pile of large, well-gnawed bones was visible.

Maddie shuddered, hoping they were sheep bones, not willing to study them too closely.

On the flagstone-covered floor, they could see traces of the chalk outline of Arazan's five-pointed star. Maddie scuffed the remnants of the outline with her foot. The chalk came away, leaving a gap.

"I'm surprised she doesn't paint it on the floor," she said, but Will shook his head.

"Eveningstar told me it has to be chalk. You have to be able to erase it. That way, the demon thinks there's a chance there might be a gap and he might be able to break through."

Maddie checked the back room of the house as Will had done.

"Nothing there," he told her.

She returned to the main room and sat on one of the stools. "She's gone," she said. "There's nothing left here. No clothes, no food. Where is she? And why did she go?"

Will shrugged. "Let's ask around. Maybe the villagers know where she's gone."

"If they'll tell us," Maddie said.

They went back out into the street and Will strode resolutely to the house next door, banging on the door with his fist. There was a pause, then it opened slowly, and a bearded face peered at them through the gap.

"What do you want?" its owner asked suspiciously.

Will jerked a thumb toward the house uphill. "Arazan," he said. "The sorceress. Where is she?"

The man's eyes dropped away from his and he shuffled his feet nervously. "Gone," he said, and slammed the door before Will could question him further.

Angrily, Will raised his fist and hammered on the door again, shaking it in the frame.

The man's voice came from inside. "Go away. I've nothing to tell you."

Will lowered his fist and exchanged an exasperated look with Maddie. He looked around and saw a woman on the opposite side of the street, watching them from her own half-open door. He paced quickly across the narrow street and caught the edge of her door before she could slam it shut in his face.

"We're looking for Arazan," he said. "Where is she?"

The woman hesitated, looking from Will to Maddie, then back again. They were grim-looking figures, in spite of Maddie's obvious youth. Swathed in their gray-and-green cloaks, cowls drawn up and heavily armed with bows and saxes, they were enough to strike fear into the villager's heart.

Although there was an even greater fear already there. Reluctantly, she decided to answer. Arazan might be more terrifying, but she wasn't here, and these two sinister characters were.

"She's gone," she said, her voice breaking.

Will hesitated, tempted to reassure her that they meant her no harm. Then he decided he'd get no information from her if she relaxed. He kept his voice grim and unfriendly.

"Where did she go?" he asked, then added, "When?"

The woman swallowed, her eyes like saucers in her head. She gestured vaguely down the hill. "Yesterday afternoon. All of them left."

"All?" Will queried. "What do you mean 'all of them'?"

"Her. And the creatures—"

"You mean her Wargals?" he snapped.

She nodded fearfully. "Yes. Vile beasts that they are. And

the wolves . . . well, two of them, anyway," she said. "Don't know what happened to the other one."

"We killed it," Will told her, and she gave him a surprised look.

"Killed it?" she quavered. "How?"

He brandished his huge bow in front of her. "I shot it," he told her shortly. It seemed easier than explaining that the horses had battered the creature half to death first.

She shook her head in wonder. "But they're from beyond the grave," she protested. "You can't kill them with mortal weapons—"

"Tell that to the wolf. It's dead on the road some ten kilometers back that way—with an arrow in it." He indicated the way they had come. The woman leaned out of the doorway and peered in the direction he had pointed, as if she might see the dead direwolf. Then she turned back to Will.

"It's dead?" she asked. "It's truly dead?"

Sensing a feeling of relief in her voice and a lessening of the terror she had exhibited so far, Will softened his tone.

"Aye. It's dead. You don't have to worry about it anymore." He paused, then added, "And we'll do the same to the other two if we can find them. Now, where did they go?"

She hesitated, wanting to believe him, wanting to know that the wolves could be killed.

"They went north," she said. "Toward the Fissure."

Will paused, considering her words. The Fissure was the massive chasm that had been spanned by Morgarath's bridge—the bridge he and Evanlyn had destroyed at the time of Morgarath's unsuccessful rebellion.

"But there's no way across the Fissure," he said. "The bridge was destroyed."

She shook her head. "There's a small bridge, a footbridge. The people built it years ago. It takes you across the Fissure to the Mountains of Rain and Night."

This was news to Will. There'd been no word of a replacement bridge being built across the Fissure, although it made sense that it could have happened in the years since the war against Morgarath. He looked at Maddie and drew her to one side. There was no need for the Celtic woman to know what they had in mind.

"I think we'd better look into this," he said in a lowered voice. Maddie nodded agreement. Then he turned back to the woman and raised his voice. "Go back inside now. And stay there. Don't tell anyone you spoke to us."

She nodded several times. The warning was unnecessary. The only person who might be interested was Arazan, and the woman had no intention of speaking to her if she could avoid it. She backed through the half-open door and shut it behind her. They heard the sound of a locking bar being dropped into place.

"What now?" Maddie asked.

Will hesitated, glancing at the sun, which was dropping in the west. "I don't want to travel by night," he said. "And I might try to contact Eveningstar at dusk. She might have been able to see what Arazan's up to." He glanced back across the road. "We could always stay in Arazan's house for the night?" he suggested.

But Maddie shook her head and shivered. "I'd rather camp somewhere," she said. "I don't want to spend a night in that house."

He nodded, understanding. "I agree. Well, let's put a few kilometers behind us before sundown. We'll find a campsite for the night, then I'll see if Eveningstar can make contact with me."

Maddie heaved a sigh of relief. For a few seconds, she had

feared that he might brush aside her objections and insist on using Arazan's house. She could still see that grisly pile of gnawed bones in her mind's eye.

"Let's get back to the horses and be on our way," Will said, and they started out down the hill together.

As they went, they were watched by dozens of eyes behind the windows of Tenruath.

20

An hour before sunset, they found a suitable campsite at a clearing beside the road. It wasn't as well concealed as their previous camps, but it was in the middle of a long, straight stretch, so Will reasoned that they would see anyone approaching them. He smiled grimly as he indicated the two horses.

"It'd take a brave attacker to try to sneak up on these two bruisers," he said.

Tug rattled his mane indignantly but didn't bother to reply otherwise.

All the same, Will decided they would have another cold camp. The smell of woodsmoke and the light of a fire would be noticeable for kilometers once night had fallen, and there was no sense in being foolhardy. Maddie had saved a flask of coffee from their midday stop, wrapping it in her bedroll to retain some warmth. Warm coffee was preferable to cold, after all. They unsaddled the horses and shared the coffee.

Will glanced at the sun, seeing it was close to the western horizon. "It's nearly sunset," he said. "I'm going to try to contact Eveningstar."

Maddie regarded him dubiously. "Is that wise?" she said. "Remember, she said Arazan might sense the two of you talking."

"I'll take the chance. Eveningstar is probably tracking the sorceress, and she may be able to tell us what she's planning—and where she's going. I won't stay in contact too long."

He moved a little away and sat, leaning back against a rock.

He closed his eyes and began to breathe deeply and evenly, trying to empty his mind as Eveningstar had directed. But inevitably, when he did so, random thoughts came creeping in. He found himself noticing the soft whistle of the wind among the rocks or trying to identify the stray sounds of insects or birds moving nearby.

And of course, the harder he tried to eliminate these thoughts, the more they intruded.

Irritably he shook himself, settled down against the rock once more and continued to try. But the stray thoughts persisted in filling his mind. Finally, he decided that, since he was hoping to have Eveningstar contact him, he might as well think about her. He concentrated on seeing her face in his mind, blotting out all other thoughts. Her calm, smiling face filled his mental vision. He held it there and breathed in and out, deeply and rhythmically.

Then he felt, rather than heard, a voice in his mind, like the silken touch of a spider's web.

Will? Are you there?

He recognized the voice as Eveningstar's. Unconsciously, he nodded, and replied, in his mind. *Yes. I'm here. I can hear you.*

The voice came again, stronger and more discernible now. *I've been trying to contact you. Is everything all right?*

Everything's fine. Arazan has gone. She's headed for the Fissure.

I know. I've been watching her. She's taken the remaining wolves with her.

What about the Wargals? Will asked.

I can't see them with her. And I can't locate them with my far-sight. Their brains are too primitive for me to find them. They could be anywhere.

What do you think she's planning? The more the conversation went on, the easier it became to communicate. Wryly, Will thought it was similar to the way he and Tug spoke to each other.

After a pause, Eveningstar answered. *If she's crossing the Fissure, she's probably heading for Morgarath's old hideout in the mountains. She may have left the Wargals to extort more silver from the surrounding Celtic villages. She'll need a lot of silver if she's going to try to subjugate Krakotomal.*

Will said nothing for a few moments, thinking over what Eveningstar had said. Apparently, the seer thought he had lost contact.

Will? Are you there?

I'm here. We'll have to follow her into the mountains.

Take care if you do. I have no idea where Morgarath's old cavern is. Do you?

No. I never went there when I was here before. We'll have to hunt for her. An idea was forming in his mind as to how they might locate Arazan's hiding place in the mountains, but he didn't articulate it now.

Remember your rosemary if you find her. And practice that banishment spell I taught you.

I'll do that.

Good luck to you, then. She paused, then added, *And Will, this had better be the last time we make contact like this, unless it's an emergency. Remember when you open your mind to me, you're also open to her, if she's searching for you.*

Will felt a small jolt of alarm at the thought that Arazan might be eavesdropping on their conversation.

Eveningstar obviously sensed his concern. *Don't worry. She's not searching now or I'd have felt it. But we need to be careful in the future.*

I'll keep it in mind. He paused, waiting to see if Eveningstar had any further advice. When none was forthcoming, he continued. *I'll be going then. I'll contact you after we've stopped her and sent her demon back to the pit.*

May your gods protect you, Will. And remember: Arazan is cunning and clever and wicked beyond belief. And so is Krakotomal. Don't underestimate either of them.

I won't. Goodbye for now, Eveningstar.

Goodbye, Will. Stay safe.

The sense of her presence faded, then was gone. Will opened his eyes and looked around the campsite. Maddie was watching him closely. He realized that his upper body was stiff and tensed, and he rolled his shoulders to ease them.

With some surprise, he saw that it was now fully dark. The sun had set and a three-quarter moon was in its first quadrant of travel, bathing the rocks in a cold, pale light.

"You made contact, I take it?" Maddie said.

He nodded wearily. "I did. How long have I been sitting here?" He rose to his feet and crossed to where his gear was piled. Picking up his canteen, he took a long swig. His throat was dry.

Maddie considered the question. "A good forty minutes. I

thought you'd fallen asleep, but then you sat up straight and started mumbling."

Will shook his head wearily. "All this mind communication is exhausting," he said.

"So, what did she say?"

"Pretty much what we've guessed. Arazan has crossed the Fissure and is heading for the mountains." Another thought occurred to him. "Oh, she said the Wargals aren't with her, so we need to keep an eye out for them. I don't want to run into them without warning."

He unrolled his bedding, spreading it out on the sandy ground. "I'm going to get some sleep. You can have first watch. Wake me in three hours."

He heard her murmur agreement. Within minutes, he was breathing deeply, fast asleep.

The night passed uneventfully. Maddie handed over the watch to Will after three hours, and he passed it back to her when his time was up. When he awoke the following morning, he found her stoking a small fire of dry deadfalls and boiling water in the coffeepot over the almost smokeless flames.

They toasted some of the flatbread they were carrying and ate it with dried meat, washing the simple meal down with coffee. Then they broke camp, rolling up their bedrolls and lashing them in place behind their saddles. Maddie kicked sand over the fire, making sure it was completely extinguished, and they rode out once more.

As the morning passed, the terrain began to change. The high cliffs on their right gradually diminished, eventually becoming a jumble of rocks and boulders barely a few meters higher than the road itself. And the yawning chasm on their left veered away from the road, until they were traveling through relatively level ground on either side.

From time to time, they saw houses and farms in the distance. But they saw no sign of people.

The sun was directly overhead, and Will had begun to look for a place to halt for their midday meal when he became aware of a faint but familiar sound behind them. The hair rose on the back of his neck as he recognized it. It was a sound from the past, from a time when he was younger than Maddie—a time of fear and dire peril.

The sound came and went on the light breeze, audible for a few seconds, then dying away, only to return slightly louder than before as the breeze gusted again.

It was a wordless, rhythmic chant, a deep, guttural sound. Ominous. Inhuman. He turned in his saddle, facing back along the road. But he saw nothing. The twisting road obscured his vision after thirty meters or so.

Still the sound came, growing noticeably stronger and more consistent, until finally Maddie became aware of it as well.

"What's that?" she asked, bringing Bumper to a halt and facing back down the road, pushing her cowl back to hear more clearly.

Will gestured toward the tumbled rocks on their right. "Get off the road and into cover," he said urgently. "That's the sound of Wargals on the move, and they're coming fast."

21

They dismounted and led the horses into the tumbled rocks and boulders beside the road. About ten meters in, they found a boulder large enough to conceal the horses behind.

"Stay here," Will admonished. Tug rattled his mane and Bumper tossed his head in acknowledgment. Then Will and Maddie made their way back toward the road, looking for a spot where they could observe the Wargals as they passed.

The boulders were gray granite, covered with patches of moss and lichen, and the Rangers' gray-and-green-mottled cloaks blended perfectly into them. Standing against the rocks, with their cloaks wrapped around them and their cowls raised, the Rangers would be virtually invisible. The only thing that would give them away was movement.

"Keep still," Will warned Maddie.

She rolled her eyes. That was the first rule of concealment, and one that had been dinned into her—sometimes by bitter experience—for years. But she said nothing.

The sound of the chanting was a constant now, no longer reliant on the vagaries of the breeze. And it was growing louder with every second as the Wargals grew closer. Will felt his heart rate quicken and suddenly he recalled that previous time—the first occasion when he had encountered a hostile, charging Wargal—when mind-numbing, gut-clenching fear had overcome him and left him frozen, unable to defend himself.

He had fought them again when he and Evanlyn—now Cassandra—had burned the massive bridge Morgarath had built across the Fissure. But in that encounter, the rush of combat hadn't given him time to think and be afraid. Since those days, he had never faced Wargals again.

Now, waiting for them, listening to their ominous chanting, he felt the old fear returning. His heartbeat quickened, matching the rhythm of their chant, and the hairs on the back of his neck stood upright in a primitive reaction so that, without realizing it, he cringed inside his cloak, in a senseless attempt to make himself smaller and less obvious.

Becoming aware of his reaction, he took a deep breath and straightened his shoulders. He was a Ranger. He had fought in scores of battles and had faced enemies infinitely more terrifying than Wargals. They were simple creatures, enslaved to the evil directions of a wicked woman.

Dangerous, yes. Vicious and implacable, yes. But mortal and vulnerable to the arrows that he and Maddie could dispatch with eye-dazzling speed. His hand strayed to the feathered ends of the arrows in his belt quiver, and he felt his heart rate steady as strength and purpose returned to him.

"All right," he murmured to himself. "Let's be having you."

The chanting was louder than ever now, and augmented by the tramp of clawed feet on the road, matching the cadence of the chant. Moving only his eyes, he looked up toward the road. He could see a five-meter length of it through a gap in the rocks and then, suddenly, the Wargals appeared.

They were marching, or rather jogging, in pairs, grunting the wordless chant as they went. There were ten of them, with an eleventh jogging at the rear.

They were all armed with short swords at their hips, and the short, heavy iron spears that were their favored weapons. They wore clumsy helmets that flared out to cover the backs of their necks, and studded leather tunics.

Two of them were carrying a large, metal-banded chest on a pole between them, and Will recalled Eveningstar's theory that they might be extorting silver from the miners to finance Arazan's activities. The Wargals were taller and leaner than the ones he remembered. Perhaps they had evolved over the intervening years. Or perhaps they were a different tribe.

The one at the rear—obviously the commander—was even taller than the others. He constantly snarled at them, urging them to keep up their speed.

Will saw that much in the time it took them to pass the gap in the rocks. Then they were hidden from sight, although the chanting continued, gradually fading as they moved farther away.

He heard Maddie release a long pent-up breath beside him, and he turned to look at her.

"Delightful creatures," she said. "I can see why you didn't want to encounter them."

"We may have to sooner or later," he said, and as Maddie began to move to fetch Bumper, he held up a hand to stop her. "I seem to recall they had an unpleasant habit of letting a couple hang back behind the main group to catch any unwary followers. We'll wait here for a few minutes."

But after several minutes had passed, it became clear that there were no Wargals acting as sweepers, and the two Rangers moved back to the road and mounted once more. The muted sound of chanting reached them still, but at least it would give them warning of where the Wargals were and prevent the Rangers overrunning them.

They kept their horses to a walk. A thinning haze of dust hung in the air above the road, marking the Wargals' passing. Ahead of them in the distance, the mountains rose black against the sky. Will gestured toward them.

"There's the Fissure," he said. "At the foot of those mountains."

In the clear air, the ominous-looking mountains appeared no more than a few kilometers away, but as they continued to ride, they seemed to grow no closer, and Maddie realized that the distance was more like ten kilometers than two or three.

Finally, the sound of chanting died away, and the dusty haze hanging over the road dissipated as the Wargals continued to increase the distance between them. Still, they rode at the alert, with their bows across their saddles and arrows ready nocked. They scanned the road ahead of them for any sign that the Wargals had stopped or were waiting in ambush.

After several hours, they came to a bend in the road. Will, who was riding a few meters ahead of Maddie, rode around it and abruptly brought Tug to a halt, backing him up and gesturing for Maddie to halt and dismount.

"We've caught up with them," he said in a low voice. Then he moved back around the bend in the road to observe. Maddie went with him, staying close to the rock face.

It soon became apparent why they had caught up with the Wargals. The creatures had reached the Fissure, but the narrow, unstable footbridge that spanned it allowed for only one at a time to cross. The motion of someone on the bridge set it swaying and lurching dangerously, so that even one Wargal crossing at a time was forced to move with extreme caution.

The footbridge consisted of short wooden slats suspended from two rope handrails, forming a V shape. It didn't look too sturdy or secure and, as they watched, the two Wargals carrying the strongbox were attempting to cross. The box was obviously too heavy for one of the beasts to carry it, so they were forced to cross together, growling and whining in fear as any uncoordinated movement set the unstable structure swaying. The other Wargals had crossed already, and the leader was still on the near side, snarling instructions at the two as they scrabbled and crept across the bridge, moving the heavy box a meter at a time between them, then clinging desperately to the rope handrails as the movement set the bridge into motion.

Eventually, after a prolonged crossing, they reached the far side and scrambled off the bridge to the safety of solid ground, dragging the strongbox clear of the edge.

Once they were safely across, the leader followed. He moved considerably faster than they had, having the luxury of holding both sides of the handrails and being unencumbered by the heavy box. Even so, he had to stop three times during the crossing, as an incautious step set the bridge swaying and its motion became wild and unpredictable. Snarling with anger, he was forced to drop into a crouch each time, clinging to the rope handrails and waiting till the pendulum movement died down and allowed him to continue.

"Are we planning to go across *that?*" Maddie asked in a whisper.

Will nodded. "Just as soon as they're out of the way."

The Wargals re-formed into their double files. The leader snapped and snarled at the two carrying the strongbox as he passed them, swinging open-handed blows at the pair as they hoisted the heavy load back onto their shoulders. Then the group set out, resuming their jogging pace and their chant as they headed for a narrow track leading up the far side of the cliffs, into the mist-shrouded Mountains of Rain and Night.

Will waited until they were out of sight as the track wound round the face of the black cliffs, then turned back toward the horses.

"All right. It's our turn."

22

"We'll never get Tug and Bumper across that," Maddie said, and Will nodded agreement.

"I didn't plan on taking them up into the mountains in any case," he said. "We'll find a spot for them on this side."

They rode back down the track, checking the terrain on either side. After a hundred meters, they found a small clearing among the rocks where the horses would be concealed from anyone passing by. Water seeped down from a seam in one of the rocks, collecting in a small pool at its base. Will scooped up a handful and tasted it. It was clean and fresh and would provide drinking water for the horses while he and Maddie were gone.

"This will do fine," he said.

They unsaddled the horses and poured out three small piles of grain onto the ground. Tug and Bumper were disciplined and well trained. They wouldn't eat all the food at once but would make it last for three days, by which time Will estimated that he and Maddie would be back.

"And if we're not?" Maddie asked.

He replied grimly: "If we're not, the horses will be the least of our worries."

They quickly prepared small packs containing supplies of beef jerky, dried fruit and flatbread, filled their canteens from the tiny spring and set out down the road toward the footbridge, first passing the remains of the huge bridge that Morgarath had built across the Fissure and which Will and Evanlyn had destroyed so many years ago. The greater part of the bridge had gone, falling into the chasm as the support ropes and timbers burned away. But the beams that had formed the support frames on either side still remained, although they were blackened and charred by the fire that Evanlyn had lit. They reared up high overhead, and Maddie let out a low whistle as she saw them.

"That must have been a big bridge," she said.

Will nodded. "It was. Morgarath planned to use it to let his army cross the Fissure and attack Duncan's forces from the rear. He had hundreds of people working on it. We got here just in time."

By contrast, the footbridge was a flimsy, unstable affair, as they had witnessed. They approached it with some misgivings.

"Wonder how long this has been here," Maddie said. She seized one of the rope handrails and pulled at it, testing its strength. The entire bridge swayed as she did.

"It looks pretty old," Will commented. "That rope doesn't look too secure."

"It doesn't seem to be rotten," Maddie said, picking at the strands of the rope with her fingers. "After all, the Wargals made it across safely, and they're heavier than you or me."

"Of course, their weight might have weakened it to the point where it's ready to give way," Will said. He was uncoiling a length of rope he had slung over his shoulder when they left the horses. Now he tied one end around his waist, looping and tying the other end over a solid rock that jutted out of the ground near the start of the footbridge.

"If the bridge does collapse, you're going to hit the wall with a heck of a thump," Maddie said.

He raised an eyebrow. "I'd hit the bottom with a much bigger one if I didn't have the rope around me," he pointed out.

Maddie stepped close to the edge and peered into the depths of the Fissure. From her position, she could see no sign of the bottom. The drop seemed to go on forever.

"True enough," she said. She started gathering up the coils of rope.

"What are you doing?" he asked.

She indicated the loose coils on the ground beside her. "I'll pay it out as you cross. No sense in you falling for the full length of the rope if the bridge does collapse," she said.

But he shook his head. "If I fall and you're hanging on to the rope, you could be dragged over the edge. I'll have the rope to stop me eventually. You won't."

She considered the point and realized he was right. He was heavier than she was and there was no solid point she could belay the rope around. She nodded and set the coils down on the ground near the beginning of the bridge.

"Just be ready to pull me back up if I need you," he said, taking the first step onto the bridge, testing the wooden slat before committing his full weight to it.

The ropes supporting the bridge creaked loudly, and the whole structure began to sway as he put his weight on it. The wooden slat beneath his foot bent alarmingly. He put his other foot on the bridge to distribute his weight over two planks and felt the first one straighten out again. But the bridge danced wildly under his weight. Gingerly, he gripped the side rails with two hands.

"This is fun," he said through gritted teeth. He edged forward, sliding one foot at a time to a new position on the bridge. No matter how hard he tried to keep his movements smooth and even, the bridge jerked and swung with each change of position and weight.

After three careful paces, he had to stop and allow the wild pendulum motion to settle down. As the swinging lessened, he inched carefully forward once more, first one foot, then the other. This time, he kept moving until he was seven or eight meters from the edge, dropping into a crouch as the bridge vibrated and lurched under him.

At ten meters, he reached the end of the rope tied around his waist. Holding the handrail with one hand, he used his other to untie the rope.

"That's as far as it goes," he said, letting the loose end fall.

Maddie hastily pulled it in. "At least the bridge seems to be solid," she said.

He shook his head. "Solid is not the way I'd describe it," he said. "It has a mind of its own."

Even though he had stopped moving across, the bridge was still swinging beneath his feet, describing a giant arc over the depths of the Fissure. And the farther he advanced toward the middle, the more pronounced the movement became.

He took a deep breath and shuffled forward another meter. The bridge, which had begun to settle down, responded in kind. The fabric of the structure creaked with the arcing movement and with the strain of supporting his weight.

He was past the midpoint now and beginning to move upward

as he climbed the far side of the sagging bridge. Becoming a little more confident, he moved more quickly, holding grimly to the handrails as his movements were translated into wider oscillations of the timber slats beneath his feet. The rope supports creaked and groaned with increasing volume.

"Take it easy!" Maddie warned, but he kept moving at the faster pace, seeing the end of the bridge coming nearer and wishing to be off it as soon as possible.

There was a splitting crack under his feet as he felt one of the slats gave way. Then he lurched downward with nothing beneath his right foot but empty space. The shattered timber slat dropped away, disappearing into the void. For a few seconds, his left foot took his entire weight and the wooden slat beneath it groaned ominously. Quickly, he transferred most of his weight to the rope side rails, heaving himself up and sliding his right foot to another slat.

Thankfully, this one was solid and it took his weight without complaint. He paused, his heart racing, his breath coming in short gasps. He waited until the bridge had settled once more, clinging grimly to the rails, his feet set far apart.

"Are you all right?" he heard Maddie's voice from the edge of the chasm. He took a deep breath before he essayed a reply, making a gigantic effort to keep his voice steady.

"I'm still here, if that's what you mean," he said, then added, "Only a few meters to go."

Resisting the temptation to hurry—which he now knew put additional strain on the aged timbers of the bridge—he crept a step at a time toward the far bank. Finally, gratefully, he felt solid rock under his reaching foot and hauled himself off the swaying spiderweb of the bridge and onto the far edge of the Fissure.

Hastily, he brought his trailing foot onto solid earth and took a few steps away from the malignant, shuddering bridge.

He became conscious that he had been holding his breath for the last few meters and let it out now in a heartfelt sigh of relief.

"Nothing to it!" he called back to Maddie, who was watching anxiously from the far side.

Coiling the rope and slinging it over her shoulder, she began to edge her way out onto the bridge, moving in the same fashion, one foot at a time. Her knuckles were white where her hands grasped the side rails. The bridge swayed wildly as she headed across. Like Will, she dropped into a crouch to maintain her balance against its unpredictable motion.

"Set your feet at the edge of the timbers," Will called to her.

She obeyed, realizing that this would lessen the likelihood of a rotten slat collapsing beneath her. It also had the effect of stabilizing her movements a little so that the swaying lessened beneath her.

As she began to sense a rhythm in the motion of the bridge, she moved more confidently, although she was careful to keep the speed of her advance down. She had seen how when Will moved faster, he seemed to put additional strain on the bridge.

The ropes groaned. The timbers creaked. But Maddie progressed steadily to the center of the bridge, then began the uphill climb on the second half. She was lighter than Will, and that meant she didn't set the bridge swaying as violently as he had. And that made the movement more even and predictable.

Without realizing it, she began to move faster as the far side came closer.

"Slow down!" Will cautioned her.

She fought against the temptation to get off the bridge

quickly, cutting her speed back, sliding one foot after another across the slats, keeping a firm hold on the handrails as she moved her feet.

She passed the gap left by the broken slat, sliding her feet with extreme caution, willing herself not to look down. Then finally, blessedly, she was at the end, and the rock edge felt unbelievably firm and steady under her feet. She lurched forward into Will's waiting arms, feeling her knees give way beneath her.

"Let's start a fire," he said. "I think we've earned a cup of coffee."

23

They found a shallow grotto in the face of the cliff, formed by a rock overhang, and made their campsite there. It would take several hours for them to climb the narrow winding track that led up to the plateau above them, and Will had no intention of doing so at night.

"I don't want to run into those Wargals in the dark," he said.

Maddie agreed wholeheartedly. "Particularly that big one who's in charge," she said.

They gathered dry branches from the small stunted shrubs that grew nearby and lit a fire to brew their coffee. Refreshed by the hot drink, Will left his small pack in the grotto and walked over to where the remnants of Morgarath's bridge seemed to crouch over the sheer drop into the Fissure.

What remained of the old beams was blackened and charred. The fire had done a thorough job destroying the huge timbers. The massive rope supports had been liberally coated with tar, which had accelerated the fire. He pointed out a few salient features to Maddie as they inspected the ruins.

"That's where your mum set the fire," he told her, indicating the few remaining timbers that had formed the footway to the bridge. "I was over there, behind those rocks."

The small outcrop of rocks that had provided cover for him had remained largely undisturbed over the intervening years. He stood, hands on hips, studying them now. They were somewhat worn down by wind and rain over the years, but still solid. Some of the smaller rocks had deteriorated or been moved by animals or men.

It seemed strange to revisit the scene after all this time, and he let his mind go back to the hopeless fight he had waged against his attackers.

"So someone was trying to stop you?" Maddie asked.

He nodded. "We were both trying to start the fire initially. But then a mixed force of Skandians and Wargals spotted us. Your mum kept working on the fire while I took cover in the rocks and held them off."

"Skandians?" said Maddie in surprise. She had heard the outline of Morgarath's rebellion but never the full details. "I thought they were our allies?"

Will shook his head. "That came later," he said. "At the time of the rebellion, they were mercenaries, working for Morgarath." He smiled bleakly at the memory. "Erak was the leader of the Skandian forces here. He actually saved me from Morgarath, refusing to hand me over. Just as well for me. Morgarath would have killed me out of hand, I have no doubt."

He walked to where the Wargals and Skandians had taken cover in the rocks, studying the ground, looking for any sign that they had been there. He had shot several Wargals, he knew, although fortunately he had not hit any of the Skandians. He thought there might be some trace of the Wargals he'd killed—bones or remnants of fur. But years of rain and wind had obliterated any sign of them. He shook his head, then stopped as he saw something half buried in the coarse sand. He stooped and picked it up, turning it over in his palm and studying it. It was metal, rusted and discolored by years of exposure to the elements, but still recognizable.

"What is it?" asked Maddie and he handed it to her, dropping it into her palm.

"It's an arrowhead. One of mine," he said. "After all these years, it's all that's left."

She handed it back, and he slipped it into his side pocket. Then he stared around the tumble of rocks and boulders, remembering that desperate fight.

"How did they capture you?" she asked.

He shrugged. "One of them threw a rock and hit me in the side of the head." Unconsciously, he raised his hand to the spot where the jagged rock had hit him. "Svengal later claimed that he was the one who did it." He smiled grimly. "Probably was. He always had a good arm for throwing. Anyway, that knocked me out cold, and they charged the bridge and captured Evanlyn. But the fire had got into the rope supports by then, and the tar went up in flames. There was no way they could put it out. They had to watch while the bridge burned, then fell into the ravine. Morgarath was furious when he heard about it. He'd based his battle plan on bringing a force across the bridge to attack the Araluen army from behind."

"Lucky for us you were here," she said.

"Lucky Evanlyn was here," he corrected her. "She got the fire started."

They began to stroll back to the grotto where they had left their packs. Maddie regarded him curiously.

"I've always wondered," she said. "You often call my mum Evanlyn. Why is that?"

"She was traveling incognito in Celtica when I first met her." He gestured across the Fissure to the other side. "Her party had been attacked by Wargals, and she'd taken her handmaid's name. The maid had been killed and your mum thought it was better if Morgarath didn't know her true identity. So I got used to calling her Evanlyn." He shrugged. "I guess the habit sort of stuck. Later on, when we traveled to Arrida and Nihon-Ja, she used the name again to conceal her real identity."

They reached the grotto and stooped as they went under the low overhang. The coals of their small fire still pulsed red in the gusting wind.

"Time for another pot of coffee before it gets dark," said Will, and knelt to rekindle the flames under their coffeepot. He cast one last look around the wide ledge where they were resting. It was quiet and deserted now. But he remembered that earlier time and shook his head thoughtfully. It was strange to return here after all these years, he thought.

They spent the night huddled in their cloaks under the rock outcrop. Once it was dark, Will extinguished their small fire. He had no concern about the smoke being sighted but the glow of even a small fire would be visible for kilometers in the darkness, and he didn't want any potential watchers being alerted to their presence.

The morning was cold and clear. They lit the fire again and had a quick breakfast, then slung their packs onto their backs and set off, heading for the track that wound up into the mountains. The towering cliffs blocked the rays of the sun. Direct sunlight wouldn't reach the platform of rock where the bridge had been built until much later in the day.

Will paused at the base of the track. He already had his bow strung. Now he selected an arrow from his quiver and nocked it, nodding for Maddie to do the same.

"Never know what we might run into on the track," he said.

She studied his choice of arrow. "Not using one of the silver warheads?"

He shook his head. "Anything we might run into will be flesh and blood, not supernatural. We know our normal arrows will deal with Wargals and direwolves. We'll save the silver arrows till we need them." He paused as a thought struck him. "Better put on our bundles of rosemary," he said, fishing his out of a pocket and hanging it around his neck. Maddie did the same.

They started up the track. It was barely a meter and a half wide and it wound up the side of the cliff. The going was steep and, before long, there was a dizzying drop to their right-hand side. As they went higher, the level ground near the old bridge became less prominent, and they found themselves peering down into the seemingly bottomless depths of the Fissure proper.

Maddie glanced over once and leaned back hurriedly. She had found herself drawn toward the huge drop.

"Don't look down," she cautioned Will.

"I wasn't planning to," he replied grimly.

They continued on, moving upward constantly. As an hour passed, they found themselves penetrating the thin clouds that clung to the higher reaches of the mountain so that visibility was reduced to less than five meters. The rocky path underfoot became slick with moisture and they picked their way carefully, slowing their pace and setting their feet solidly with each step they took. A slip or a fall here, with the yawning drop less than a meter away, could prove fatal.

"Any idea where Morgarath's old headquarters might be?" Maddie asked.

Will shook his head. "I was never taken to them. I was with the Skandians, who had a camp among the rocks up on the plateau. Once we reach the top, we'll scout around until we find a Wargal patrol. Then we'll follow them and hope they lead us to wherever Arazan might be."

"Will she have the Wargals patrolling?" Maddie asked. Will's plan seemed a little on the thin side to her.

"I would if I were her. And she's no fool. She knows we're about. She may not know that we've crossed the Fissure after her, but she won't take the risk that we haven't. So she'll have her Wargals keeping an eye out for us, just in case."

"And her direwolves," Maddie added ominously.

Will nodded. "Yes. Them too. Still, if they're patrolling, it gives us a chance to whittle down their numbers."

"That's the positive view of it," she said.

He smiled. "The glass is always half full for me."

The cloud cover grew thicker and visibility was reduced the higher they went. Maddie's calf and thigh muscles were burning with the effort of climbing hour after hour. Without realizing it, she was grunting quietly with the effort of each upward step.

"Do you want to rest for a while?" Will asked, as he became aware of the fact.

But she shook her head. "Let's keep going. If I stop now, I

may never get started again—and I don't fancy spending the rest of the day on this track."

He said nothing, but continued climbing. His leg muscles were shrieking from the constant effort as well, but he had years of training and conditioning behind him, and he continued to place one foot ahead of the other in a steady rhythm. After another half hour, he reached his hand behind him, gesturing for her to stop. She leaned against the rock wall to her left, breathing deeply, as he continued ahead of her, disappearing into the swirling mist around them.

After a few minutes, he reappeared, beckoning for her to continue.

"Come on," he said. "We've reached the top."

24

THE PLATEAU THEY EMERGED ONTO WAS A DESOLATE WORLD of tumbled boulders and sandy, gravelly soil. There were trees here, but they were stunted and twisted, blown by the ever-present wind so that they leaned to the side. None of them was more than three meters in height. It appeared that the wind kept them that way. They were scattered among the rocks, as if the conditions on the plateau prevented them from growing closely together. Their branches and trunks were clad in gnarled, gray bark, and their foliage—what little there was of it—was a dull gray-green. In spite of the constant dampness, the trees looked to be dry and brittle—possibly as a result of the prevailing wind.

Altogether, it was an inhospitable place and one that seemed appropriate for the sinister activity Arazan was planning. Maddie looked around at the grim rocks and twisted trees and shuddered.

"What a place!" she said with a note of distaste in her voice.

Will nodded agreement. "When you think of the people who've made it home, like Morgarath and Arazan, it seems totally suited to them."

"So, where to now?" Maddie asked.

Will hesitated, studying the surrounding landscape. From

ground level, it was difficult to see any distance. The rocks and boulders blocked his line of sight. He moved toward the nearest outcrop and climbed onto it. The outlook was no better from a more elevated position. The jumble of rocks stretched out in all directions, and he could see no sign of any form of habitation.

"I know Morgarath had his headquarters up here in a series of caves," he said. "But I never saw where they were." He scrambled back down to ground level and indicated the trail leading away among the rocks. "Our best bet would be to follow the track inland and see where it leads us."

She frowned. "I had hoped for a more positive plan than that," she said. "That sounds distinctly like 'suck it and see'—as the cook used to tell us when we asked what he was serving for dinner."

"Sounds like a wise cook." Will grinned. "That way, you couldn't really complain that he'd given you any false expectations. Besides," he added, "with any luck we'll run into some of the Wargals and we can follow them."

"You have a strange idea of luck," Maddie said.

Will pointed to the narrow trail leading away from the cliff edge. "Let's go," he said, and led the way inland. Maddie followed a few meters behind him. Each of them had an arrow nocked and ready.

They trudged on. The path wound in and out among the boulders, and at no time could they see more than thirty meters in front of them—most of the time even less. Maddie felt her heart rate accelerate. They would have little warning if they encountered any of Arazan's creatures. The Wargals would be bad enough, but if they ran into a direwolf they'd have to shoot fast. Will seemed to be having the same thoughts.

"Keep your eyes open," he warned her. His voice was tense. "And your ears," he added. "The Wargals tend to make a lot of noise when they're on the move."

She pushed back the cowl of her cloak so as to hear better. But there was no sound audible other than the keening wind as it blew among the rocks and the stunted trees.

They were on a short stretch of the track when the Wargals suddenly appeared from around a bend ahead of them.

There were three of the creatures, all armed with spears and wearing metal-studded leather jerkins and the distinctive helmets that the Rangers had seen before. The Wargals stopped with a grunt of surprise, taken aback by the unexpected sighting of the two Rangers.

Will and Maddie were startled but were quicker to recover than the Wargals. As the three beasts began to charge forward in their peculiar, hopping gait, the two bows came up and each of them snapped off a shot. They had discussed this sort of situation many times and knew the danger of both shooting at the same target. Accordingly, each of them selected a target corresponding to their relative positions—Will to the left and Maddie to the right. Both shots went home, and the two Wargals tumbled onto the sandy track. The third, seeing his companions so quickly put out of action, turned and began to run for his life.

He screamed in pain as Will's second shot struck him on the lower leg, causing him to stumble, so that Maddie's next arrow sailed over his head. Then, before either of the Rangers could shoot again, he was round the bend in the track and out of sight.

"After him!" said Will, and they set off at a run to catch him. The track at this stage was a series of short, zigzagging sections, so when they reached the bend, they were just in time to see him disappear round the next turn. Maddie pulled ahead of Will, ignoring his warning that the Wargal might turn back on her, and pounded down the track, nocking an arrow to her bowstring as she went.

She flew around the next turn, just in time to see the Wargal disappear once more. As she ran after him, straining for more speed, she could see blood from his wound staining the ground. There seemed to be a lot of it and she wondered how long it would be before loss of blood slowed him down. All she knew was that they had to stop him before he escaped and raised the alarm that they were on the plateau.

Another bend and, once again, she was just in time to see the creature disappear from sight ahead of her. She had raised her bow at the fleeting sight of him, but he was gone before she could shoot, and the action cost her several hard-won meters. She could hear him now, uttering shrill yelps of pain and fear as he tried to escape. Behind her, she heard Will's feet pounding down the track, but he was too far behind to be of any assistance.

I hope the Wargal stays on the track, she thought desperately. If he had any sense, he would have struck off into the jumble of rocks and boulders and trees where she could so easily lose sight of him. But he was a simple creature and was ruled by the primitive urge to escape, to flee, to continue running from the nemesis behind him. *Fight or flight*, she thought, the saying leaping into her mind as she tried for more speed. Her hip, always a weak point, ached, and she began to limp as she ran.

Rounding another bend, she found herself facing an extended fifty-meter length of straight track.

The Wargal, obviously realizing he would be exposed to her arrows for a longer time, had switched tactics. He stopped mid-track and turned back, his spear held in both hands as he lunged at her.

She snapped off a shot, but it clanged against the beast's metal helmet, the arrow skating away into the rocks beside the track. Then the Wargal, moving with incredible speed, was upon her, with the square-tipped head of the spear reaching for her.

She was moving too fast to sidestep the attack. Instead, she dived forward, going under the spear and rolling past the Wargal so that she came to her feet several meters behind him.

She faced him now, scrabbling to pluck another arrow from her quiver. But her cloak had become entangled with it as she rolled, and she fumbled desperately.

Fortunately for her, the Wargal's injury slowed his recovery as he spun around to attack her. She felt a second of panic as he lunged at her once more with the spear, keeping its point low, expecting her to dive under it again.

But this time she was able to dodge to one side, and the spear clanged off the rock wall beside her. Cursing the cloak that was impeding her, she jabbed the tip of her bow at the Wargal's eyes, forcing him to shy away and lose balance. He staggered on the injured leg, then set himself again. The long, canine muzzle opened and a savage growl emerged. She saw the yellow fangs bared at her, the hatred in his bloodshot eyes, and realized the bow was no use to her now. She tossed it to one side and drew her saxe, conscious that it offered an inadequate defense against the heavy spear.

She deflected the next thrust with her saxe, nearly losing her grip on the weapon as it made ringing contact with the spear.

The Wargal jabbed at her again, and she leapt back, narrowly avoiding his attack. He snarled again and followed up, jabbing at her, forcing her to leap backward, away from the spear. He slashed at the saxe, trying to smash it from her grip. The impact left her right hand and arm numb. Then he struck again, bringing the iron spear down onto the blade of the saxe, and ripping it from her grasp.

As her saxe clanged onto the rocky ground, she saw a momentary gleam of triumph in the Wargal's eyes. Knowing she was disarmed, he abandoned haste and slowly began to advance on her, thrusting and jabbing with the spear, driving her backward a step at a time.

Until, in a moment of utter despair, she felt the solid rock wall at her back and knew there was no more room to retreat.

The Wargal paused. He bared his fangs again and uttered another blood-chilling snarl. There was no mercy, no pity in his eyes. He drew the spear back for one final lunge.

Then jerked forward, a look of surprise replacing the triumphant snarl on his face as Will's arrow slammed into his back, at a range of five meters and with all the force of his massive longbow behind it.

The spear dropped from the Wargal's lifeless fingers, clanging on the rocky path. Still trying to comprehend what had happened to him, the creature sagged and dropped to his knees, then tumbled forward, facedown.

Maddie drew in a huge, shuddering breath as she looked at the lifeless, horrific form only two meters away from her. She looked up to see Will at the bend in the track, another arrow ready and nocked on his bow, the bow itself half-drawn in case the Wargal was shamming. Then, realizing it was dead, Will released the tension and replaced the arrow in the quiver at his belt.

Maddie, suddenly weak at the knees, leaned against the rough, head-high rocks at the side of the track.

"You certainly took your time," she said.

25

ARAZAN PACED THE STONE FLOOR OF HER CHAMBERS, A WORRIED frown on her face. She sensed danger, but she couldn't pinpoint the source. Something was blocking her farsight, and she suspected Eveningstar's influence. The woman had extensive knowledge of the charms and talismans that could interfere with Arazan's ability to view far-distant objects or people. In the past few months, she had become an increasingly annoying presence. One day, thought Arazan, she would have to be dealt with. She wondered how effective Eveningstar's powers might be against a demon like Krakotomal, and a cruel smile crossed her features. The demon had enormous powers, and once Arazan had brought him under her control, Eveningstar would be in serious danger. Arazan looked forward to that final confrontation, which was now only a short time away. Her hold over the demon was growing, and soon it would be time to bring him across into this world.

She tuned her senses now to her direwolves. She could see them curled up among the rocks on the top of the plateau, outside the series of caves she had appropriated for her quarters. They seemed relaxed and unworried.

Next, she searched for her Wargals. Marko, the semi-intelligent leader of her tribe, was patrolling the flat, open area outside the caves. In the old days, Morgarath's forces had used it as a drilling ground. Marko sensed her attention and straightened, looking around warily. She moved on to the rest of the Wargals. There were twelve of them—thirteen including Marko—in the tribe she had brought under her control, and she had set them to patrolling the plateau, in search of any approaching enemies. She cast her vision wider to find them. They were searching in groups of three and were scattered across the plateau.

She found the first group almost immediately. They had headed farther inland and were scouring the rocky wasteland in search of intruders. From their relaxed manner, they had obviously found nobody, although they had encountered several Wargals from other tribes—tribes that had not been influenced by Arazan and were continuing to live their normal peaceful lives among the rocks and caves. Startled by Arazan's aggressive subjects, they had fled in terror from their cousins.

The second trio took a little longer to locate. They had gone south and were some five kilometers away from the cave complex Arazan had taken over. They too seemed to have found no sign of interlopers on the plateau. They were scrambling across the rocky terrain in their habitual loping gait, searching among the boulders and caves that abounded there.

So far, she thought, there seemed to be no reason for her sense of impending danger, yet Arazan hadn't survived all these years by ignoring her premonitions and instincts. She continued to seek her other Wargals.

Three more had gone east and she found them almost immediately. There was little chance of danger coming from that direction, she knew. The only access to the top of the plateau was via Three Step Pass, and that was a narrow and difficult track that led up from the plains far below. In half a dozen places, the pass had been blocked by rockfalls, set in place after the final battle between Morgarath's and Duncan's forces so many years ago and making it virtually impassable. She quickly ascertained that the three Wargals who had traveled east had encountered no threat to her presence.

She cast her mind out to the remaining three. They had headed west, back toward the cliffs leading up from the Fissure—the route she and her followers had taken to reach the plateau.

There was no sign of them.

She concentrated more fiercely, directing her thoughts and her senses toward the western section of the plateau. But again, she found nothing.

Alarm bells went off in her mind. This was a problem—a serious problem. The Wargals were too simpleminded to shield their presence from her senses. She should be able to sense them, and visualize them, easily. Perhaps they had moved south of the point where the precipitous track led back down to the Fissure. She concentrated her thoughts in that direction but again came up empty.

Perhaps, she thought, they had gone back down to the large level space where the footbridge now spanned the Fissure. She searched that location but again found nothing.

She brought her awareness back to the top of the track and began to probe the terrain leading inland, searching in vain for a sight of the three missing Wargals.

But there was nothing there.

Wait!

A brief, fleeting sense of . . . something, or somebody, registered in her mind, then was gone. It lasted only a moment, and she tried desperately to recapture it, but to no avail. It had been someone, she was sure. Someone who had no business up here on the plateau.

Her thoughts flashed to the fleeting glimpse she had caught of a young woman when she had sensed Eveningstar spying on her some days ago. The image had been there for a fraction of a second, then gone. But now, as she searched the jumbled rocks at the top of the plateau, she became convinced that it was this girl she was sensing.

She groaned in frustration as she strove to find the intruder. She was sure there was somebody there. She could sense the masking power that prevented her from seeing her—or him. As her mental vision passed over a section of the rocky wasteland, she sensed a blurring effect, a loss of focus, a distinct sensation that something was blocking her thoughts, preventing her from seeing a full picture of what was there.

The mental effort involved in trying to pierce that fog was enormous. Perspiration broke out on her brow and soaked the dark robe that she wore.

Arazan clutched a hand to her forehead and moaned. A massive, pounding headache struck her and she staggered, clutching at the back of a chair for support as she nearly fell to the stone floor of the cave. Then the effort became too great, and she felt her knees giving way. She just managed to collapse onto the chair before she fell. She sagged in the chair, her body limp, and the image of the plateau outside was shattered and vanished from her mind.

Utterly drained by the vast mental effort she had been

expending, she managed to rise from the chair and stagger to her bed, falling across it and dropping into a deep, exhausted sleep.

"What was that?" Will said, stopping in his tracks and raising his head to search for the presence he had just felt. It was as if a gossamer hand had brushed across his consciousness, invading his mind and trying to pierce through to the core of his soul.

Maddie had felt the same invasive sensation and she looked at him, her eyes wide-open with alarm. "You felt it too?" she asked.

"It's Arazan," he said, reaching for the bundle of rosemary hanging round his neck and touching it. "She's searching for us."

"Can she see us?" Maddie asked fearfully. She too touched the rosemary as if it were a talisman that could ward off evil. "Did she see us?"

Will shook his head. "I don't . . . think . . . so," he said. He let his mind relax, searching again for that phantom touch, that sense of being observed by an alien presence in his mind. But there was nothing there. "She's gone now. But if she could see us, my guess is it was a pretty murky vision. I got a sense that some-one was *trying* to identify me, but they hadn't managed it."

"But if she's searching for us," Maddie said, "that means she knows we're here. She knows we're coming for her."

Will considered that idea for a few seconds before replying. "Not necessarily us," he said. "She may sense that somebody is here. But if Eveningstar's right, she couldn't see us or identify us."

"*If* Eveningstar's right," Maddie repeated. "Who's to say that's the case? We're dealing with a lot of unknowns here."

Will shrugged. "She's been right with most of what she's told us." A thought struck him. "Maybe this is because of those three

Wargals we fought," he said. Maddie cocked her head in a question, and he elaborated. "We know Arazan has a mental link with them. Maybe she's sensed that they're dead. Or maybe she can't sense them now that they *are* dead. That could be what has her alarmed."

"So what do we do now?" Maddie asked.

Will nodded toward the center of the plateau. "We keep going. We keep heading inland. Morgarath's old headquarters must be somewhere in that direction. And, at least now that she's not looking for us, we'll have a better chance of surprising her."

"Maybe you could try to contact Eveningstar again and see what she advises?" Maddie suggested.

Will considered the idea for a few seconds, but then shook his head decisively. "I could. But if I try to open up my mind to Eveningstar, I might make myself visible to Arazan as well."

Maddie shuddered. "Then don't try that, for pity's sake," she said quickly. She shook her head. "All this mental vision stuff is so complicated. I prefer a problem that I can handle with a well-aimed arrow."

Will sighed in agreement. "Me too. But odds are, before too long, we'll get our wish in that direction. Now let's get moving again. We've got a few hours of daylight left, and we still have to find Morgarath's old lair."

26

Night found them still searching the rocky wasteland for Morgarath's old lair. They were covering ground slowly, conscious of the need to move carefully and avoid confronting any of Arazan's minions. As they sat among the boulders a few meters from the rough track, Maddie contemplated the prospect of another cold, fireless camp with displeasure.

"A person could get heartily sick of cold dried beef and flatbread very quickly," she observed.

Will shrugged fatalistically. In his life, he had spent too many uncomfortable nights like this to be concerned by one more. "At least we've got coffee," he said. They had boiled water at their midday halt and kept a pot of hot coffee wrapped in a blanket to retain its warmth.

Maddie looked into her mug now, frowning heavily. "Lukewarm coffee," she pointed out. "I sometimes think you can taste the grounds more when it's lukewarm than when it's cold."

"You may be right. But it's still preferable to cold water," he told her. She grunted with displeasure and shifted her shoulders against the rocky outcrop she was leaning against.

"So what's the plan for tomorrow?" she asked, more for something to say. She already knew what they'd be doing when the sun rose again. But Will surprised her.

"It strikes me that we should try to even the odds a little," he said.

She roused herself to look at him. "How do you mean?"

"Well, we're a little outnumbered as it is. Arazan has at least ten Wargals and two direwolves to hunt for us. And avoiding them is slowing us down. Maybe we should go on the offensive and whittle down their numbers. I'm not happy about just sitting back and waiting for those direwolves to find us."

"It would be a pleasant change to see them being nervous about moving around up here," she said thoughtfully. "But won't that alert Arazan to the fact that we're here?"

Will considered the point, then replied. "She already suspects it. We felt that earlier today. And it's obvious that she's set her Wargals to search for us—or at least, for someone."

Several times that afternoon, they had encountered groups of Wargals scouring the plateau. While they had no trouble concealing themselves from the creatures, it set their nerves on edge having to continually take cover. And it slowed their progress as well.

"Plus, sooner or later, we're going to have to confront her and this demon of hers. When the time comes, I'd rather do it without having to worry about Wargals and wolves as well."

"I like the way you're thinking," Maddie said.

Will smiled at her. "In that case, you can take the first watch," he told her, pulling his cloak up around his shoulders and settling down on the rocky ground, moving around until he found a more or less comfortable position.

"I didn't like it that much," Maddie told him.

But there was no reply. He was already asleep.

The following morning, they put their new plan into action. They had been traveling for about an hour when they heard the familiar grunting and shuffling of clawed feet on the rocky trail that told them a group of Wargals was in the vicinity. The two Rangers melted into the rocks beside the trail, pulling their cloaks closer around them to conceal them from the beasts' vision.

Peering from inside her cowl, Maddie pressed herself against a large rock outcrop and watched the three Wargals shuffle past in their peculiar loping fashion. As they moved past, she was conscious of another movement close by her and she saw Will step out from behind a rock, his bow in his left hand, an arrow nocked to the string.

The three Wargals had reached the next bend in the narrow track when he drew back and released, before freezing to the side of the rock once more, his cloak wrapped around him.

The speeding arrow slammed into the rearmost Wargal, sending him staggering forward with a cry of pain and shock. Then he dropped facedown onto the rocky ground, sliding a meter or so with the momentum of the arrow.

His two companions reacted with shock and panic at the sight of him. They backed against the rocks at the side of the track, their weapons raised, their eyes searching around them.

It would have been a simple matter for Will and Maddie to shoot down the remaining two, but that wasn't the idea.

"I want them frightened," Will had told Maddie. "I want them reluctant to search for us and ready to disobey Arazan. That way, she'll have to set her wolves after us."

"Are we sure we want that?" Maddie asked uncertainly.

He nodded. "We'll have to face them sooner or later. I'd rather we can pick the time and the place."

Now panic was setting in among the two surviving Wargals. Their fearful chattering rose to a peak as they tried to see where the attack had come from. But there was no sign of their attackers among the grim, gray rocks and mist. Nervously, they began to retrace their steps along the track, heading back the way they had come. They passed the spot where Will and Maddie stood motionless and almost invisible against the rocks, then, struck by the same instinctive panic, they ran, leaping and skipping back down the track.

Within a few seconds, the sound of their fearful retreat faded away, masked by the boulders on all sides.

Will's expression was somber as he studied the still form of the Wargal he had shot. He retrieved his arrow, moving carefully until he was sure that the fearsome beast was dead and not shamming.

"I don't like having to kill them," he said. "They're simple creatures, and it's not their fault. They're under Arazan's influence."

Maddie didn't share his regret. To her, the Wargals were fearsome, pitiless beasts who wouldn't hesitate to kill or maim her if they had the chance. She'd felt a fierce surge of satisfaction when she saw them running away, chattering in fear.

"It's not our fault either," she said callously. "Blame Arazan if you want to blame anyone. But remember, there's nine of them and only two of us."

Will nodded and they resumed their path inland, staying close to the rock walls that lined the track, checking around each bend and twist in the track to make sure the way was clear before proceeding.

Now that they had decided to go on the offensive, they were able to move faster. Instead of trying to avoid the Wargals, they were seeking them out. They still moved cautiously, but with more purpose, following the tracks left by the primitive creatures.

The path was covered in sand and gravel and small rocks, and the Wargals left a clear trail for them to follow. Their clumsy clawed feet and violent hopping movements left marks in the sand and gravel that were easy to see and to follow—particularly for two skilled trackers.

The Wargals led them in a southwesterly direction, which Will estimated to be taking them toward the central point of the plateau. He nodded to himself. That made sense. He had always assumed that Morgarath's old headquarters lay toward the middle of the wide plateau, and the farther they went, the more the ground opened up, so that the wild tumble of rocks and boulders became more evenly spaced, with clear areas becoming more apparent.

Now, mounting the taller rocks in the area, they could see much farther. By midafternoon, Will could make out a low-lying range of hills on the horizon.

"I'll wager that's where Morgarath had his cave," he said quietly.

Maddie scrambled up onto the rock beside him to look for herself. She could see the dark line of a set of low cliffs on the very edge of the horizon. Instinctively, she touched the bundle of rosemary hanging round her neck on its leather thong.

Will saw the movement and smiled. "It's still there. She can't see us," he said.

Maddie nodded, then inclined her head toward the track ahead of them. "Maybe not. But he can," she said.

In the open ground, some forty meters away from them, a lone direwolf had appeared.

As they watched, it sniffed the air experimentally, turning its long muzzle from one side to another. Will turned his head so that he could feel the breeze playing on his cheek. It was a gentle-enough breath of air, but it was blowing from them to the huge carnivore.

There was no doubt it could scent them—although Maddie seemed to be wrong. The massive beast couldn't yet see them.

It snarled, baring its overlong canine fangs. Then it threw back its head and let out a full-blown howl, the blood-chilling sound echoing among the rocks and boulders that strewed the plateau.

Maddie reached carefully for the quiver at her hip and sensed Will doing the same as he nocked an arrow to his bow string.

"Looks like it's time to even the odds a little," he said.

27

The two bows released within a second of each other, the double *THRUM* they made overlapping into one extended sound. As might be expected, Will was the first to shoot, and his arrow, propelled by the extra power of his bow, pulled away from Maddie's lighter shaft as they both sped toward the direwolf.

It slammed into the creature's chest a second before Maddie's shot reached its target.

The massive impact threw the direwolf back onto its rear legs, raising its body off the ground and laying it open for Maddie's shot.

The wolf had barely begun to recoil from the impact of Will's arrow when Maddie's sliced into it, piercing the unprotected lower body of the creature and penetrating deep into its chest cavity.

As it did so, Will's arrow, boring remorselessly on, lanced into the wolf's massive heart and dropped the creature stone dead to the gravelly ground beneath it.

In retrospect, it seemed a deceptively simple matter to dispatch such a fearsome enemy. It was dead within five seconds of Maddie's first sighting it. But the seeming ease with which they killed the monster didn't take into account the training and discipline of the two archers.

Either shot would have proved fatal, but the speed and accuracy of the two shots was remarkable. Nine out of ten archers, faced with the horrific sight of a direwolf, would have panicked and jerked at the string as they released so that the arrow would have either wounded the direwolf or missed clean. As he watched the animal slump to the ground in an ever-widening pool of its own dark blood, Will recalled his first encounter with Morgarath's Wargals. The sight of the relentless, bloodthirsty creatures seeking him out had frozen him to the spot in blind panic so that when he did shoot, his shot was rushed and missed entirely.

And the direwolf was a much more fearsome creature than any Wargal. He glanced sideways at Maddie, noting that while her face was pale with tension, she already had a second arrow nocked and ready to shoot if necessary.

"Nice work," he said quietly. Not for the first time, he reflected on her courage and steadiness in tight situations. Then he thought of her parents—Cassandra and Horace—and nodded to himself. *No wonder*, he thought.

Maddie finally took her eyes off the dead wolf as she let her arrow down and replaced it in her quiver. "You hit it first," she said.

He smiled. *So I should*, he thought, *I've years more experience in these things.*

"Maybe," he told her. "But you finished it."

She shook her head. They both knew that the direwolf had died a moment after Will's arrow had slammed into its chest. Still, Will wasn't prepared to argue. If his shot had missed, Maddie's would have completed the task, and he was glad to have that kind of backup—steady and unfaltering under pressure.

"Either way," he said, "it's one less that we'll have to deal with before we're through."

They scrambled down from their vantage point on the rocks and approached the wolf cautiously, alert for any sign that it was trying to lure them closer. But as they came up to it, they could see it was dead. Its eyes were open and glazed, and its tongue lolled out of its mouth over the long, yellow canines. There was no sign of life in the creature.

"Ugly brutes, aren't they?" Maddie said.

Will nodded. "But efficient for their task," he said, "which is killing."

Their arrows weren't worth retrieving. Maddie's had bent as it penetrated the wolf's chest cavity and Will's was saturated with blood for almost two-thirds of its length. Neither would shoot accurately again.

They left the massive furry body where it lay. Soon the crows and kites would begin to gather overhead to feast on its flesh. There was no point in trying to conceal it. The more Wargals that saw it and became nervous and afraid of the people who had killed it, the better.

Will gestured in the direction where they had seen the dark line on the horizon.

"Let's move out," he said. "We're burning daylight."

Maddie smiled at him. "Been a long time since you've told me that," she said.

As they trudged on across the windswept plateau, Will reflected on the difference he had noted between Arazan's Wargals and those that Morgarath had enslaved so many years ago.

Morgarath's Wargals had been characterized by the fact that, once committed to battle, they would continue to fight ruthlessly and relentlessly until the contest was settled—one way or another. They would give their lives if need be, without ever deviating from the path they had been set on. They were unaffected by growing casualties among their own ranks and uncaring about their own fate or that of their comrades. It was this grim determination that had made them such a dangerous force. Once set upon an attack, only death would stop them. Their only weakness was their obsessive fear of horses.

Yet now, in comparison, Will and Maddie had seen Arazan's Wargals reduced to chattering fear by the sudden death of one of their comrades. They lacked that relentless commitment that had characterized Morgarath's army. They were savage, to be sure. But they could be terrified and demoralized by a determined and well-trained enemy.

Perhaps, he thought, Arazan hadn't had the years that Morgarath had enjoyed to bend them to his will and dull their sensibilities, turning them into remorseless automatons who knew only two possible results—victory or death. Or perhaps Arazan, evil and malicious as she might be, was nowhere near as malignant as the dark lord who had gone before her. He felt a shudder run through him.

Maddie noticed the movement. "Problem?" she asked.

"Someone just walked on my grave."

She frowned at him. "Poor choice of words, under the circumstances," she told him.

He smiled wanly. "I was just thinking about Morgarath and how he'd trained his Wargals to be utterly pitiless and fearless," he explained. "Arazan's troops don't have the same commitment or mindless determination."

She shook her head. "They'll do for me," she said. "I certainly wouldn't want them any worse than they are."

"I wasn't complaining," Will said mildly.

Maddie replied, with some force. "Besides, Morgarath didn't have direwolves as well, did he?"

"He did not. Although to be accurate, neither does Arazan now. She has only one left, and thank Gorlog for that."

"Let's not forget that demon she's trying to raise. It strikes me he could be worse than any number of Wargals or direwolves."

"That's a cheerful thought," said Will. Once again, his hand went to the bundle of rosemary hanging around his neck. It was getting to be a habit, he thought.

The going became easier as they progressed farther toward the center of the plateau. The terrain was still marked by extensive rock fields and tumbled boulders, but the impediments became more widely dispersed, the ground more open, and Will and Maddie were less dependent on narrow trails winding through the rocks.

They sighted Wargal search parties on two more occasions during the afternoon but they were far in the distance and moving away from the two Rangers. They showed no sign of having sighted them. Once or twice, Will felt that same cobweb-like touch on his consciousness as Arazan's farsight passed over him. Each time, he glanced quickly at Maddie and saw that she had felt it too.

"Think of something else," he said quickly. They were both conscious of the fact that if they thought directly about Arazan, they might open themselves to her arcane mind-probing.

But Maddie was skilled now in keeping the image of the witch out of her imagination. As she felt the tendrils of Arazan's farsight brush her mind, she immediately filled her thoughts with images of Bumper—thinking of the times they had faced danger

together and how comforting his thoughts and courage and loy-
alty had been to her on so many occasions over the past few
years. It proved to be an ideal distraction and she found herself
smiling at the thought of her loyal little horse. So effective was
it as a distraction that, without meaning to, she turned to Will
and asked a question.

"Does Tug talk to you?" she blurted out.

Will paused in midstride, turning toward her. "Talk to me?"
he said. "How do you mean?"

She shrugged awkwardly. She hadn't meant to ask the question, but now it was out in the open. "I often hear Bumper in my
mind. I hear what he's thinking. Do you do that with Tug?"

There was a long pause and then he slowly smiled and nodded. "I wasn't sure if I was the only one," he said. "But I'm pretty
sure all Rangers talk to their horses."

"And their horses talk back?" she persisted. She was relieved
to hear his admission. There had been times when she had wondered whether she was totally sane when she heard Bumper's
thoughts in her mind.

"And their horses talk back."

28

IT WAS LATE AFTERNOON WHEN THEY FINALLY REACHED THE low line of cliffs they had seen on the horizon.

The going had become easier, with the ground opening up from the initial tumbled mass of rocks and boulders, so that they could follow a more direct route. They came to the edge of an open plain, which had been cleared of obstacles. Beyond that, the cliffs rose to a height of some twenty meters. They could see a long, open gallery along the face of the cliffs, three or four meters from ground level.

In the foreground, set on the open field between them and the cliff line, the Wargals had built their hovels and shelters, using old scraps of timber and branches from the scrubby trees that dotted the plateau. There was no sign of the remaining direwolf, or of Arazan herself. But the taller lead Wargal, whose name Eveningstar had told them was Marko, appeared, emerging from the cave in the cliff face and prowling through the Wargal camp. There were three Wargals in the camp. The others, presumably, were still out patrolling.

Will and Maddie found a small outcrop of rocks where they

could conceal themselves while they observed Arazan's head-quarters.

"What now?" Maddie asked.

Will gestured toward the open gallery running along the face of the cliff. "I'm guessing that's where you-know-who has her base," he said. They had agreed not to use Arazan's name, for fear that it might open them to her farsight. "We'll keep an eye on that and see if we can figure out where she is and what she's up to."

"So, more sitting and waiting and watching?" Maddie asked.

Will nodded. "That's what a Ranger does most of the time," he told her.

She grunted in reply. He was right, she knew. A large part of her training had been aimed at helping her achieve this sort of patient watchfulness. But that didn't mean she enjoyed it. She preferred the excitement of action.

The rest of the day rolled on without anything notable happening. Occasionally, one or two of the Wargals would stir themselves and prowl about their small camp. Just before sunset, the remaining members of the tribe returned to the campsite.

It was only a few minutes later that there was movement at the entrance to the caves. The Wargals all turned to face it, moving into a protective huddle, shifting their feet and whining nervously.

Maddie and Will followed their gaze, and the two Rangers stiffened in surprise as a figure emerged from the shadows. It was a woman, short and heavyset, clad in a shapeless black robe embroidered in silver thread with strange designs: half moons, five-pointed stars, circles and triangles. Her hair was gray and unkempt, framing a broad, florid face in greasy tangles. Her face itself was set in an ill-featured scowl.

The two Rangers exchanged a look. Even though they had glimpsed her only briefly through Eveningstar's viewing portal, they recognized her instantly.

Arazan. Maddie mouthed the word at Will, and he nodded. He felt a grim sense of satisfaction to be finally viewing his quarry in the flesh.

The sorceress moved from the cave entrance to the Wargals' camp. Padding close behind her was an enormous shape—the remaining direwolf. It was gray, with a black head and shoulders, and it followed her as she approached the assembled Wargals. The strange creatures continued their whining and shuffling. It was obvious that Arazan ruled by fear, not affection of any kind.

Marko barked a series of orders at the Wargals, and they shuffled into a ragged line on the open ground, standing respectfully while Arazan paced up and down before them, stopping from time to time to lean forward and peer closely into a Wargal's eyes as she came level with it.

"What's she doing?" Maddie whispered.

Will leaned toward her and replied in a matching soft tone. "She's interrogating them. Remember, she speaks to them with her mind. She doesn't need words. My guess is she's asking if they've seen any sign of us during the afternoon."

From their nervous attitudes and Arazan's growing annoyance, it was apparent that the Wargals answered her queries in the negative. Marko barked angrily at them as they did. His mistress was frustrated by the lack of information they were passing on, and that sense of frustration communicated itself to him. But no matter how he snarled, they continued with their negative reports.

Two of the Wargals huddled behind their companions, trying to avoid Arazan's gaze. Watching them, Maddie realized they must be the two who had led them to the camp. Arazan stopped in front of them and leaned forward intently. The Wargals cringed away from her, shaking their heads in negative movements.

She's realized one of them is missing, Maddie thought.

Arazan continued her silent probing and questioning for several minutes. But the two Wargals continued to cringe away from her, shaking their heads repeatedly.

The direwolf, curled up against a large rock at the edge of the open ground, watched impassively.

Finally, Arazan turned her back on the two recalcitrant Wargals with a furious gesture of dismissal. She snapped a command to Marko. The dominant Wargal barked a series of orders, and most of the others slunk back to their shelters, heads down and moving slowly. Three of them, however, followed Arazan as she strode angrily back toward the caves.

From their hiding place in the rocks, Will and Maddie watched as the small group disappeared into the entrance. A minute or so later, they could make out four shapes moving along the elevated gallery. Arazan preceded the Wargals, carrying a burning torch to light her way. Eventually, she and the others disappeared into a cavern at the end of the gallery.

Will nodded toward the gallery. "Those three must be her guards," he said, and Maddie nodded agreement.

Maddie and Will waited for half an hour while the last of the daylight died. They could see a glow of light from the gallery in the cliff face, but no further movement. The Wargals gathered around a central fire and began to roast meat on sticks held out to the flames. The direwolf, showing no more interest in his companions, settled down to sleep, his huge muzzle laying on his forepaws. Marko, after seizing some of the meat roasted by the other Wargals, gulped it down and retired to the shelter of his own hovel.

Will nudged Maddie and pointed with his chin toward the entrance to the cave.

"Come on. Time we saw what she's up to," he said.

They left their bows and quivers hidden among the rocks. The weapons were too long and cumbersome for covert movement in the confines of a cave. Using the cover of the shadows and the intermittent rock outcrops, they crept stealthily toward the cliffs. They were both trained in moving silently and undetected, and five minutes later they were sheltering in the dark entrance at ground level. Will paused, looking back at the Wargal encampment. There was no sign of alarm, no indication that they had been seen or heard. The massive direwolf continued to doze and Marko remained in his shelter, out of sight. Satisfied that they hadn't been observed, Will led the way into the cave complex.

A short flight of stairs cut out of the rock led up to the gallery where they had observed Arazan. They mounted the steps, Will leading the way, his hand on the hilt of his saxe. They reached the gallery level and looked out on the Wargals' small camp. Nothing was moving there. Will gestured for Maddie to follow him and set out along the gallery, crouching low so as to avoid being seen from below. Maddie followed a few meters behind him. Their soft-soled boots made no sound on the rock floor of the gallery, and they made their way toward a dim glow of light some thirty meters away. Here the open gallery ended and continued as a tunnel through the rock. The walls were lined with burning torches in sconces set into the rock wall, and Maddie and Will moved silently from one to another, their shadows like huge spiders on the tunnel walls.

They moved cautiously, conscious that at any time they could encounter the three Wargals who had accompanied Arazan. But the way was clear.

Five meters along, another tunnel opened off to the side, leading farther into the cliffs. Will paused for a moment, studying it, then shook his head and continued along the main tunnel.

After another thirty meters, they rounded a bend and could see a spill of light coming from a cave in front of them. Moving carefully, pressed against the rock wall, Will made his way to a lighted entrance. Maddie, after waiting for him to stop, moved up to join him.

Together, they peered cautiously round the rough doorway and were confronted by a large cave that opened up before them.

The three Wargals lay or sat on the rock floor in the foreground. Beyond them, a bed and a table and chairs furnished the cave, which was some ten meters by seven, with a ceiling roughly five meters high. A large fireplace was built into the far wall, and it was from here that the light was coming. A fire burned warmly in the grate, and Arazan's dark-robed figure was seated before it, with her back to them. She was rocking back and forth in her chair, crooning softly to herself. The words were indecipherable— they were in some ancient dialect that neither of the Rangers recognized.

For a moment, Maddie found herself wishing that they had brought their bows.

It would be a simple matter to shoot the necromancer where she sat and be rid of her once and for all. Then she suppressed the thought. It wasn't the way Will operated, she knew. He would never shoot anyone in cold blood. But he might well seek to take her prisoner.

But as they were, with only their knives, that wasn't a possibility. The three Wargal guards were fully armed, with spears and short swords, and all three were wearing leather jerkins set with metal plates as armor. Any attempt to take Arazan prisoner would mean they would have to fight and subdue the well-armed creatures, and the odds were stacked against the Rangers in such a confrontation. Even if they did succeed in overpowering Arazan's guards, the rest of the Wargals and the remaining direwolf were outside the cave, between them and freedom. And they'd be alerted by the sound of fighting in the cave—or by Arazan's mental link with them. It would be virtually impossible to make it past them with Arazan as a prisoner.

In addition, they needed to make sure that Arazan hadn't yet summoned the demon Krakotomal. If that had happened, they would need the witch to send him back to the other side. Killing her might well release him, setting him free to wander the world, unchecked and uncontrolled.

Suddenly, Arazan sat up straight, and Maddie felt the familiar brush of her senses searching for her. Hurriedly, she filled her mind with images of Bumper, dispelling any thought of Arazan. She clasped her hand around the bunch of rosemary at her throat, not daring to breathe. After several long seconds, the witch subsided and relaxed back in her chair. The strange singing began again.

Maddie started as Will's hand touched her arm. She looked at him and he jerked his head back down the tunnel behind them. Silently, she moved away from the entrance to Arazan's cave and they headed back the way they had come, with Will once again in the lead.

She expected him to head back to the stairs and the cave entrance, but when they reached the side tunnel they had bypassed previously, he stopped and indicated they should enter it. He leaned closer to her and whispered.

"This may be where she does her summoning and spell casting." And he set out down the gloomy passageway. The walls were closer here and the ceiling was lower, barely half a meter above their heads. Instinctively, they moved in a crouch, their way lit by more torches set along the walls.

Will paused to study one of them. It was burning freely and still coated with pitch to maintain the flames.

"They've been lit recently," he said. "They won't need replacing for an hour or so."

That was good news. Maddie didn't like this shadowy tunnel. If any of Arazan's assistants chose to enter it—to replace the torches, for example—she and Will would be trapped here.

They wound on, going farther into the cliff. Then, unexpectedly, they rounded a bend in the tunnel and came upon Arazan's main chamber.

29

ARAZAN'S INNER SANCTUM WAS A MASSIVE NATURAL CAVERN. It covered an area approximately ten meters by ten meters, with the roof arching up high above them, in some places lost in the shadows. Where they could see it, it was at least twelve meters high.

The floor space had been cleared and large rocks and boulders were piled up all around. Will studied them quickly, seeing that they provided numerous hiding places from where he and Maddie would be able to look down on the floor of the cavern.

The floor itself was solid rock, worn smooth over the years. To one side, the now-familiar shape of a five-pointed star inside a circle was drawn on the floor. Maddie moved toward it and leaned down to touch the white outline. Her fingers came away smeared with fine powder. The design was drawn in chalk dust, she realized. In one or two places, the outline was smudged or broken where footsteps had disturbed the powder.

Will went down on one knee to study the design more closely.

"This is her pentacle," he told her. "It's how she keeps safe when she's summoning the demon. He can't penetrate the circle, so long as the outline is unbroken. But she has to redraw it each time she tries to summon him. And it can't be permanent.

"Remember what Eveningstar told us. The demon has to believe that there's a chance that he can attack the person summoning him. Before she tries another summons, she'll go over the pentacle and fill in any gaps in the outline."

There were half a dozen small sacks on the floor to one side of the pentacle. Will picked one up and untied the cord fastening its neck. He poured a small amount of chalk dust out onto his hand. He studied it for a few seconds, then dusted his hand off. He retied the sack and slipped it into his pocket.

"What do you want that for?" Maddie asked.

He made an uncertain gesture. "Oh, just thinking of something," he said. He was beginning to have the first inkling of an idea about how to combat Arazan and the demon, but it wasn't anywhere near fully formed yet, and he was reluctant to discuss it at this point.

He walked around the circle of chalk dust, studying the ground inside. Then he turned and looked across the vast, gloomy cavern. A few meters away, in the center of the floor, the stone was marked and stained black.

"Eveningstar said it can take several attempts to summon a demon. We saw one of them the other night."

Maddie shuddered. "Yes. I remember. Not something I want to see again."

Will shrugged. "We may have to. Apparently, each time, the summoner's hold over the demon becomes stronger, until eventually he crosses over the barrier between his world and ours and materializes here, under her control." He pointed to the blackened circle on the stone. "That's probably where she summons him."

He dropped to one knee and rubbed his hand on the darkened stone. His fingers came away blackened.

"It's been burned," he said, half to himself. He stood up again and scanned the walls of the cavern, taking in the tumbled rocks and the crannies and crevices between them. "Plenty of hiding places," he said softly.

Maddie followed his gaze. "You're not thinking of hiding in here while she tries to bring that . . . *thing* into the world, are you?" she said in a horrified voice.

He shrugged again. "It might be the best way to deal with her—and it," he said. "We've got our silver-headed arrows to kill the demon. And I'm sure they'll be just as effective on the witch. If we can catch them together, we can put an end to the whole business. Eveningstar taught me a banishing spell for the demon. If we could just work out a way to get him trapped inside the pentacle with her, that could do the trick."

Maddie shook her head slowly. "You can't be serious," she said. "I don't want to come within twenty kilometers of that beast. The direwolves and Wargals are bad enough, but he's positively"—she paused, looking for the right word, then found it—"unworldly."

"I know what you mean. But if we can let her summon him, then break her concentration and control over him, he may well turn on her and take her back with him. That way, we'd get rid of both of them for good."

"And how exactly do you plan to do that?" she challenged.

He opened his mouth to reply, then closed it again. "Haven't *quite* worked that out yet," he admitted. He looked around the surrounding walls of rocks and boulders. "But we could hide up in there, and our rosemary will shield us from her senses."

"What about the demon's senses? Won't he know we're here?" Maddie asked.

He chewed his bottom lip thoughtfully. "I shouldn't think so," he said finally. "If it blocks Arazan from knowing we're here, it should work on him as well."

"*Should*," Maddie repeated. "It seems you're taking a lot for granted here."

She'd witnessed Arazan's earlier attempt at controlling the demon. She was horrified at the prospect of being in the same room as the two of them if the witch repeated the attempt— particularly if she succeeded next time.

Will looked at her for several moments, understanding the dread she was feeling.

"I can do it by myself if you want," he said.

But she shook her head wearily. "No. I can't let you do that. I'll help you—"

She didn't finish the sentence. He held up a hand to stop, her, his ear cocked toward the passageway by which they'd entered.

"Someone's coming," he said.

They both listened. They could hear the unmistakable hopping, scraping sound of a Wargal's clawed feet on the rock floor of the tunnel. Will looked quickly around. There was no other exit from the cavern, only the tunnel by which they'd come. And that was now blocked. There was no way out. They'd have to hide. He gestured toward the steep rock walls around them.

"Up here!" he said. "Get out of sight."

They scrambled toward the piled-up rocks and boulders, climbing quickly away from the cave floor until they were four or five meters above the pentacle. The higher they went, the deeper the shadows grew. As the noise of approaching footsteps—or claw steps—grew louder, they crouched behind two large rocks, their cloaks drawn around them, the bundles of rosemary clutched tight in their hands. Utter silence and absolute stillness were now their best defenses, Maddie knew. She calmed her breathing, making it deep and even. But she could do nothing about the pounding of her heart. It felt loud enough to alert anyone within twenty meters of her hiding place.

A Wargal bounded into the cavern, in that ungainly fashion they had. She drew in her breath sharply. It was Marko, the leader of the Wargal tribe, the semi-intelligent creature who was the most dangerous of all the Wargals. He peered suspiciously around the cavern, searching for any sign of interlopers. Maddie had no way of knowing if he sensed a foreign presence or if he was perpetually on the alert. Then he turned back to the entrance to the tunnel.

"Aw clear," he rasped in his mutilated voice.

A few seconds later, the dumpy, black-clad figure of Arazan entered behind him. She paused for a second or two, sweeping her gaze around the cave. Then she relaxed and moved farther inside, heading for the smeared pentacle. Marko prowled around the circumference of the room.

She fixed her gaze on him and frowned in concentration, but as she did, he waved one hand in a negative motion.

"No think," he growled. "Speak."

She let out a short laugh. "Of course, my trusty boy," she said indulgently. "You want to practice your speech. It makes you feel superior to your kinfolk, doesn't it?"

"Margo speag," the Wargal said in his thick, distorted voice.

"Very well, then. We'll use words, not thoughts," she told him.

Marko nodded several times, obviously pleased with her agreement. She moved toward the pentacle, studying the scuffed chalk lines and frowning.

"Hmmm. Made a mess here last time," she said, more to herself than to the Wargal. He, for his part, stepped closer to her and looked at the pentacle as well, his head tilted to one side, for all the world like a curious dog.

"I'll have to redraw these lines," she said. "Tomorrow night I'm bringing Krakotomal across into this world."

30

Concealed among the rocks, Maddie and Will watched as Arazan repaired the broken chalk line of the pentacle. She moved carefully around the outer circle, holding one of the bags of chalk dust in her hands.

Whenever she came to a point in the circle that was scuffed or smeared or broken, she would carefully replenish it with chalk dust from the bag, stooping so as to be close to the work and making sure that any gap was completely filled. Once she had made sure of the outer circle, she carefully stepped over it and checked the chalk lines that drew the inner five-pointed star, pausing from time to time to let the white dust trickle out from the neck of the sack she held in her hands.

She worked with consummate care, checking and double-checking the chalk lines, humming to herself as she went. At one time she turned to Marko, who was watching her intently.

"Got to make sure, Marko," she said, chuckling throatily. "One little gap, and Krakotomal will be in here with me."

The Wargal grunted but made no other comment.

Eventually, she was done. Maddie estimated that it must be past two o'clock in the morning when the sorceress finally straightened, tied the cord around the neck of the now-depleted sack of chalk dust and nodded to herself in satisfaction.

"All done," she said. "Now we wait for midnight tomorrow to bring Krakotomal under my power."

Then, with the Wargal trailing behind her, she turned and left the cavern, the sound of her footsteps, and the scraping noise of Marko's claws on the rocks, fading away into the distance.

The two Rangers waited for several minutes after they could no longer hear her. Then Will let out a long pent-up breath.

"So, tomorrow night," he said. "If she's successful, we'll have her and Krakotomal together in the room."

"And then what?" Maddie asked.

Will shrugged. "I'm working on that," he said. "But we'll need to be ready and back in place at least an hour before midnight."

Maddie looked around the gloomy cavern. The torches were beginning to burn down and the light was fitful and uneven.

"I guess we could stay here and wait," she suggested. "That way there'll be less chance that we're spotted moving around outside."

But Will shook his head. "No. There are still things I need. And besides, we're going to want our bows tomorrow night."

He moved silently to the entrance to the passageway that led away from the cavern. Pausing, he cocked his head to listen for at least a minute. But aside from the slight sound of the wind blowing down the tunnel from outside, there was nothing. He nodded his head toward the dimly lit passageway.

"Let's get out of here," he said.

They regained their hiding place in the rocks outside the cave complex and settled down, their cloaks wrapped around them.

There was no sound from the Wargal camp or from the gallery in the cliffs. An hour before first light, they saw the direwolf rise silently from its resting place before the burned-out fire. It padded off into the shadows. Half an hour later, it returned and settled down in its resting place again with a soft grunt.

Dawn rose and they watched as the Wargals stirred. One of them hobbled out to the fire and laid fresh kindling over the smoking coals, then fanned the flames to life so that the kindling caught fire. As the flames flickered up, he added progressively heavier pieces of wood until the fire was blazing once more. The smell of woodsmoke filled the air. Maddie, who had been awakened by the movement in the Wargal camp, thought ruefully of hot coffee. She sipped at her cold water canteen instead. It was a poor substitute.

The day rolled on. The Wargals toasted bread and meat by the fire for their breakfast. Then half of them donned their leather armor, buckled on their sword belts and hefted their spears before heading off on patrol. The remainder settled down to rest. After several hours, the patrol returned to the campsite. Four of the others went out on patrol, searching in vain for the two Rangers who were concealed in the rocks less than fifty meters away.

There was no sign of Arazan during the day. Maddie assumed she was resting. Presumably, summoning the demon would be a physically and mentally exhausting task.

The direwolf spent the day curled up a few meters from the Wargal camp. Occasionally, it would rouse itself and lope off for several hundred meters, scouting the immediate area around the caves. Then it would return and flop down once more, falling asleep within a few minutes.

Around the middle of the afternoon, Marko emerged from his shelter and loped across to the gallery entrance. They saw his form moving along the open gallery toward Arazan's chambers. When he had gone, the other Wargals seemed to relax a little. The afternoon patrol returned as the sun was sinking over the horizon and the Wargals began to prepare their evening meal.

During the day, Will had rummaged through his pack, searching for items he might use that night. His plan was beginning to form more fully now, and he set out a small clay bowl from their cooking equipment, along with his water canteen—still three-quarters full—and the sack of chalk powder he had taken from the cavern the night before. Maddie watched him curiously, but he made no attempt to explain what he had in mind. Probably just as well, she thought. They were too close to the Wargal camp to indulge in idle chatter. She assumed he would tell her when the time was right.

Marko returned from the gallery and took the negative reports from the patrols that had gone out during the day. He growled angrily in response, then dismissed his tribe and returned to his shelter. A short while later, one of the Wargals took him a bowl of the food they had prepared. The others gathered around the fireplace, helping themselves to the cookpot and eating voraciously.

The meat stew simmering over the Wargals' campfire sent out a tantalizing, savory smell on the cold evening air. For Will and Maddie, it was dried beef and cold water once again.

Will and Maddie watched and waited as the sun went down and the Wargals relaxed around their fire. When it was fully dark, the strange beasts began to retire to their shelters until only two were left. Eventually, one rose and piled fresh wood on the fire so that the flames leapt up and burning cinders whirled up into the night sky. Then the two Wargals turned away and crept into their respective shelters as a fine, misting rain began to fall, its drops hissing into the leaping flames.

Will waited for ten minutes, making sure the Wargals were settled down for the night, then he collected the gear he had laid out during the afternoon and gestured to Maddie. He clipped his quiver full of arrows to his belt, pushing a wad of sheepskin down among the arrows to hold them firmly and prevent their rattling as he moved, then picked up his bow. Tonight, they would need their bows, and now that they had ascertained that the way to the cavern was relatively clear, they knew the long weapons wouldn't be an encumbrance on the way. He gestured for Maddie to do the same.

"Time to go," he whispered, and led the way through the rocks toward the entrance to the cave complex. He moved cautiously, slipping from one group of shadows to the next and keeping a wary eye on Marko's shelter in case the Wargal leader might emerge.

There was no sign of Marko in the time it took for Will and Maddie to make their furtive way to the cave entrance. They paused in the shadows, waiting and listening. But there was no sound of alarm from the Wargal camp or from the sleeping direwolf.

Will touched Maddie on the shoulder and, crouching low, led the way into the cave complex and up the steps to the open gallery above.

They paused at the top as Will waited and listened for any sign of movement. But there was nothing other than the constant sighing of the wind along the passages. Signaling for Maddie to follow, he set out along the gallery, staying low so that his movement wouldn't be visible from the Wargal camp. When they reached the side tunnel that branched off to Arazan's inner chamber, he paused again, listening, then led the way inland.

As before, the narrow corridor was lit by flaring torches set in sconces in the rock wall. There was no sight or sound of anyone ahead of them and, within a few minutes, they reached the entrance to the massive cavern where Arazan planned to summon the demon.

Will paused before entering, peering carefully around to make sure Arazan wasn't yet in place. But the cavern was empty, and he went forward, with Maddie a few meters behind him. He stopped in the middle of the vast floor space, looking round at the rocks lining the walls and up at the ceiling, high above. Then he crossed to the chalked pentacle at the far side of the cavern.

The design was still freshly outlined from Arazan's work the night before. He studied it carefully, looking for any sign of a gap or a flaw in the chalk lines that formed the star and the circle around it. There was none and he nodded to himself, then moved to the point nearest the jumble of rocks that lined the walls, studying the rocks themselves for a spot that would suit his purposes.

After a few minutes, he found what he was looking for. A small pile of rocks at floor level lay close to the outline of the circle, less than a meter away. And the uneven floor sloped down toward the circle. Above the small pile, larger boulders were tumbled together, with a narrow gap between them that offered a place of concealment.

"This will do nicely," he said.

31

WILL REACHED INTO HIS JACKET POCKET AND PRODUCED THE clay jar he'd placed there earlier, then he unstoppered his water bottle and proceeded to fill the jar with water. It held about three-quarters of a liter. Maddie watched curiously. She was tempted to query him, but she knew through long habit that he would tell her what he was doing when he was ready to—and not before.

Carefully, he built up a small pile of rocks half a meter above the chalk line and set the jar on top of them, measuring the angle and distance between them with his eye, moving the jar until he was happy with its position. Then he sat back on his heels.

Eventually, Maddie couldn't wait any longer.

"So?" she said. "What are you doing?"

"I'll be waiting in the rocks above here," he said, indicating the hiding place he had seen earlier. "I want you on the other side of the cavern. Once Arazan has raised Krakotomal, I'll give a signal, and I want you to shatter this jar with a shot from your sling. Can you manage that all right?"

She studied the distance to the far side of the cavern, then looked back at the clay jar. "I take it the idea is to break the jar so that the water in it runs down the rocks to the chalk line?" she said.

He nodded. "That's right. The water should wash away a section of the chalk and give Krakotomal an entry point into the pentacle, with Arazan."

"It'll also give him an exit point, won't it? Even if he deals with Arazan, we'll be setting him free into the world."

But Will shook his head and indicated the rocky slope above the pentacle. "I'll be hiding up there," he said, "with this bag of chalk dust I picked up last night." He produced the small sack he had taken from a pile of similar bags. "While Krakotomal and Arazan are fighting each other, I'll dash down and repair the gap in the pentacle. They'll both be trapped inside."

Maddie let out a low whistle. "That's pretty risky," she said. "You'll be taking an awful chance."

Will shrugged. "I should be safe enough. It'll only take a few seconds, and they'll be distracted with each other. Besides, I'll have my rosemary necklace to conceal me."

Maddie pursed her lips doubtfully. "That conceals you from Arazan," she said. "Does it work against Krakotomal?"

Her teacher hesitated, then replied. "It should," he said. "I hope it will."

"It'd better," Maddie said with some feeling. "But it only prevents Arazan sensing your presence. It won't stop her actually *seeing* you, and you'll be out in full view. And it won't stop the demon."

"It'll only be for a few seconds," he said. "Once the chalk line is restored, the demon will be trapped inside the pentacle—along with Arazan."

There was a long pause. Maddie was very unhappy with the plan. It seemed full of risks to her, and it was based on too many suppositions: If she could break the jar. If the water breached the pentacle. If Will could repair it in time to trap the demon inside it.

"So let's assume it all goes to plan," she said, "and you have the demon trapped in here. What do we do next? D'you think he's simply going to go home to Demonland—or wherever it is he comes from?"

"I assume he'll destroy Arazan," he said. "From what Eveningstar said, demons are always very keen to get the upper hand over the person who summons them and tries to control them. Once he's done that, Eveningstar gave me a spell of banishment, remember? I'll use that to return him to wherever he came from. That way, we'll be rid of Arazan and the demon in one hit."

"You're taking a lot for granted," Maddie told him.

He shrugged. "I can't think of a better way to handle it. Can you?"

"We could use our silver-tipped arrows and simply shoot him when he appears," Maddie suggested, but he shook his head.

"We don't know that they'll stop him on their own," Will told her. "My way, we're using their own powers and rituals to get rid of the two of them. And if it does go wrong, we can always fall back on the silver arrows."

Again, a long silence fell over the two of them. As Maddie considered his plan, she realized he might be right. And she could always stand by with a silver-tipped arrow in case things didn't go according to plan. She knew from bitter experience how often things *didn't* go according to plan.

Finally, she let out a long sigh. "All right," she said. "But I've got another problem."

Will motioned for her to explain further, and she pointed to the jar full of water sitting on the little pile of rocks.

"You want me to break the jar with a slingshot," she said, "and let the water run down onto the pentacle." He nodded and she continued. "Problem is, I'll be shooting from across the room there." She indicated the far side of the cavern, where Will had suggested she might hide.

"It'll be safer for you there," he said. "The farther away from the pentacle you are, the better." He paused, then asked, "Are you worried about hitting the jar?"

He was surprised at the thought. He knew she was an expert shot with the sling. Hitting the jar, even in the uncertain light of the cavern, should be a simple task for her. But she shook her head.

"No. I can hit it all right," she said. "But, if I shoot from over there, I'm just as likely to knock the jar over backward, so the water doesn't run downhill to the chalk line. It could just splash all over the rocks behind it."

Will studied the situation and saw that she was right. The sling delivered its shot with devastating power. It was quite likely that if it hit the jar full on, it would smash it backward, and the water inside would go everywhere.

Before he could speak, Maddie continued. "I'd be better to hit it with a ricochet shot, so I'm knocking it forward."

Will frowned, looking at the jar balanced on its pile of small rocks. "How do you—"

Maddie cut him off. "Hold this," she said, leaning forward to remove the jar and handing it to him. Then she searched through the rubble to find a rock approximately the same size as the jar. She placed it on the pile, then rummaged around once more until she found a larger piece, roughly square in section and flat-sided. She placed this behind the rock she had just put in position, taking a few seconds to adjust its angle until she was satisfied with it.

Will watched her curiously, gradually realizing what she had in mind. "You're planning to bounce off the flat rock and knock it forward?"

She nodded. "Just stand clear," she said. He moved to one side while she crossed the cavern to the spot where she would be concealed. She studied the angle of the shot while she unwound the sling around her wrist and shook it out. Then she loaded a lead shot into the pouch.

Her eyes narrowed as she took her throwing position. Her left foot was advanced half a meter, her right foot behind it. Her right shoulder dropped as she let the loaded sling dangle down behind her. Her left hand pointed out toward the target. She concentrated on her target. The light in the cavern was poor and unsteady, but she'd made tougher shots than this before.

Then she whipped the loaded sling up and over, stepping forward into the shot as she did so and releasing the leather thong at the moment when it would hurl the shot on its way.

There was a brief whizzing noise as the lead projectile flashed across the cavern, then a dull smacking sound as it smashed into the flat rock she had placed in position. The rock was firmly supported by a large boulder behind it and the shot ricocheted back from it, angling down to strike the smaller rock that had replaced the clay jar. The smaller rock seemed to leap in the air, flying forward toward the pentacle. It landed on the stone floor with a clatter, a few centimeters from the chalk line.

"That ought to do it," Maddie said.

Will inclined his head. "Great shot."

She smiled at him. "Well, you know, I'm not just a pretty face," she told him. Then she crossed the cavern again to study the flat rock she had used to ricochet her shot. The impact had put it somewhat out of line and she adjusted it, checking the sight line repeatedly to ensure it was properly positioned. Then she gestured for Will to replace the clay jar full of water.

He did so, conscious once again how fortunate he was to have such a capable and talented assistant. She was young, he thought, barely out of her teens. But he knew she would go on to be one of the greats among the ranks of the Ranger Corps.

Maddie made a final inspection of the jar and the flat rock, looking back across the room to ensure she was happy with the angle of the shot.

"Now all we need is for Arazan and her demon to show up," she said.

Will smiled at her. "I can hardly wait," he said.

32

The two Rangers used the time before Arazan arrived to select two good hiding places in the rocks above the cavern floor, on opposite sides of the cavern. They settled down to make themselves as comfortable as possible while they waited.

Maddie unslung her bow and placed it within easy reach of her position. Then she laid the sling out on a large rock nearby, along with two lead shot from her pouch. One should be all she would need, she thought, but it was always wise to have another in reserve.

Once she was settled, she looked across the cavern to the spot where she knew Will was concealed. She was pleased that she could see no sign of him—not that she expected to. He was a master of concealment, after all, like all Rangers.

She pulled up the cowl of her cloak, bringing it forward to put her face in its shadow, and then wrapped the gray-green cloak around her. It blended almost perfectly into the gray rocks of the cavern and she knew that, so long as she remained still, she would not be seen by the witch.

She touched the bundle of rosemary around her neck—a movement that was becoming something of a habit. Reassured that it was there and would hide her from the witch's senses, she settled down to wait.

The minutes dragged on. Somewhere in the cavern, water was dripping down onto a rock. The sound seemed unnaturally loud now that there was no other movement. After a while, she felt a cramp forming in her left thigh. Carefully, making sure she made no noise, she eased her position to relieve the muscle. She hoped the cramp wouldn't get worse. Once Arazan was in the cavern, there'd be no movement possible. Movement would cause noise, and noise would reveal her to the witch. Gently, she rubbed the tensed-up muscle in her leg.

I never get cramps, she thought angrily. *Why now, of all times?*

She knew that if she moved her leg in the wrong direction trying to ease the cramp, she could easily set off an agonizing spasm. Perversely, the temptation to move became stronger and stronger. But she resisted it, and gradually, the knotted muscle lost its tension and the cramp disappeared. And none too soon, as she heard a slight noise in the passageway leading into the cavern.

Arazan was coming.

The hunched, black-clad figure of the witch appeared suddenly in the entrance way. She paused, peering suspiciously around the dimly lit area. But the masking effect of the rosemary bundles held firm, and she sensed no foreign presence in the cave. After a few seconds, she advanced into the cavern and crossed to the pentacle, walking slowly around it, checking to make sure that the chalk lines were unbroken. Maddie held her breath as the sorceress seemed to pause near the rock pile where Will was concealed. Would she notice the clay water jar among the rocks? Or the flat rock positioned to reflect Maddie's shot? The more Maddie thought about it, the more unnatural the positioning of that flat rock was.

But the jar, made of unglazed clay, blended into the rocky background, and Arazan moved on farther around the pentacle. Maddie let go a long-held breath in a silent sigh of relief.

For a moment, she wondered why Arazan was alone and not accompanied by her faithful Marko. But she assumed that he would be in danger if he were present when the demon was summoned. Or perhaps he might be a distraction to Arazan? Whatever the reason, Maddie was relieved that the Wargal wasn't present.

Finally, Arazan completed her inspection of the pentacle. She moved to the spot in the center of the floor where the stone was charred and marked with soot. She poured a small quantity of green powder onto the stone floor, spreading it out with her foot so that it formed a rough circle. Presumably, this would be the place where Krakotomal would materialize.

Satisfied, she moved back to the pentacle. Holding the hem of her robe high to avoid scuffing the chalk line, she stepped over it and took up a position in the center of the star. She sank to her knees on the stone floor, then sat back on her heels. She was facing toward the charred spot on the floor and Maddie could see her face clearly.

Arazan closed her eyes and began to chant in a low voice. The words were indecipherable to Maddie, but she sensed the witch was using some foreign language.

The chanting grew gradually louder until the hoarse voice of the sorceress began to fill the cavern and echo off the rocks. Now Maddie could hear clearly, and she realized that her supposition was correct. Arazan was chanting in a language unknown to her.

"Ikab jandlar remko. Ikab jandlar simet. Ikab jandlar, jandlar ikab."

The words resonated through the cavern. They seemed to pulse in Maddie's head, becoming louder and louder with each passing utterance. Yet she was sure that Arazan hadn't actually increased her volume. The words of the chant seemed to have their own penetrative quality that blocked out other sounds and became dominant. Maddie felt the beginnings of a headache behind her eyes.

Then, on the floor of the cavern, something moved.

"Ikab jandlar remko. Ikab jandlar simet. Ikab jandlar, jandlar ikab."

A small curl of green smoke arose from the scorched spot on the floor, rising slowly into the air and disappearing in the darkness of the upper regions of the cavern.

As Arazan continued to chant, Maddie became conscious of another sound behind her voice: It was a deep-throated growl, a terrifying sound full of menace and threat. A growl that came from nowhere and yet began to resonate with the witch's chanting.

"Ikab jandlar remko. Ikab jandlar simet. Ikab jandlar, jandlar ikab."

The thin curl of green smoke became thicker and heavier. Instead of rising into the air, it began to spread out along the stone floor above the charred spot, appearing almost liquid in the way it flowed across the floor of the cavern, yet coalescing so that its edges became thicker and higher, until it was almost a meter high and filling a circle two meters wide.

As it pulsed and roiled within itself, Maddie became aware of the smell of sulfur.

And again she heard that terrifying, otherworldly growl that grew louder and louder and joined with the hoarse-voiced chanting of the sorceress. And now the roaring and the chanting and the vile smell filled the cavern. Maddie cringed back among the rocks in fear, her eyes riveted on the thick green cloud that hung so close to the floor.

Then something—something indefinable, something unrecognizable yet totally malignant—began to form inside the green cloud.

It came and went. One second, she was sure she could see a shape. Then it disappeared into the smoke once more. But then it would return, more clearly defined than before, only to melt away again.

Each time it appeared, it was clearer and more visible. And, each time, it hung in the smoke cloud for a few seconds longer than the time before, so that Maddie began to recognize shapes more clearly.

And the roaring and the chanting continued, fighting with each other for dominance.

Now she caught a glimpse of a green, scaly serpent's body. Then it was gone. And then she thought she saw wings—wings like those of a bat, but much larger and covered in the same green scales.

And now a face—but a face unlike any she had seen before. It was formed in flat planes and hard angles, with two glowing eyes and jaws that opened to reveal multiple rows of sharp fangs.

Then it was gone, fading back into the green smoke.

The chanting changed, and she could recognize at least one word among the others, and that word was a name that sent pulses of fear racing through her.

"*Abazur tomak Krakotomal! Abazur Krakotomal, indira jabla Krakotomal.*"

Krakotomal! The name of the demon. And as Arazan chanted the name, the sights Maddie had half seen through the green smoke cloud began to form more fully.

The body of a serpent, with huge, batlike wings covered in scales. And that dreadful, horrifying face, jaws open to reveal fangs like knives.

As she watched she saw it take shape, reared up on thick, short, heavily clawed rear legs, using the wings to support its upper body. The eyes were two triangular slits in the horrific face, burning with hatred as the creature writhed under the flail of Arazan's chanting.

"*Abazur tomak Krakotomal! Abazur Krakotomal, indira jabla Krakotomal.*"

The creature roared in anger and pain and tried to lunge toward the crouching figure inside the pentacle. Then its voice, a horrifying deep voice that grated on the senses, boomed out.

"Leave me alone! Leave me, I say!"

Maddie sat upright, shocked, as she realized she could understand the words. She saw that the last of the oily smoke had disappeared, leaving only the green-black scaled shape of the demon in the center of the cavern floor. It was four meters long and two high, and snarled and snapped in the direction of the pentacle and the chanting sorceress.

"*Abazur tomak Krakotomal! Abazur Krakotomal, indira jabla Krakotomal.*"

"Leave me! Let me be!"

Now, for the first time, Arazan ceased her chanting and spoke. "Krakotomal! You are mine. I command you to obey!"

33

THE HAIR STOOD UP ON THE BACK OF MADDIE'S NECK AS THE demon howled in anguish, defying the constant chanting of the sorceress.

"Leave me be, mortal!" the demon roared, but Arazan continued her chanting.

"Abazur tomak Krakotomal! Abazur Krakotomal, indira jabla Krakotomal."

The huge, horrific body swayed back and forth in a futile attempt to break Arazan's hold. Then Arazan switched to plain language.

"You are mine to command, Krakotomal. You *will* obey me."

The only reply was an inarticulate roar of fury as the demon tried vainly to break the sorceress's grip on him.

"Obey! Obey me!" Arazan screamed.

"No-o-o-o-o-o! Leave me be!" the demon replied.

Maddie crouched, spellbound by the continuing contest between the two.

"On your knees! Kneel to me and do my bidding!"

The command echoed around the cavern, and Krakotomal

shuffled backward a few paces, then slowly began to fall to his knees as Arazan commanded. But the movement was accompanied by a roar of such rage and anguish that the sound of it set Maddie's skin tingling with fear. Never had she witnessed such a savage and all-encompassing struggle of wills.

"On your knees and pay homage to me, beast!" Arazan ordered.

Slowly, the demon came to his knees, his head swinging back and forth in a vain attempt to break the necromancer's control over him. But the spell and the pentacle held firm, and he was forced to crouch, his head down on the stone floor of the cavern, his giant bat wings spread out either side for balance.

"Tell me I am your master! Tell me you will obey!"

"No-o-o-o-o!" The word grated out in the monster's cracked tones. But now Maddie could sense another note in it—a note of reluctant and furious submission. Krakotomal would submit to his summoner. He would obey her. But he would hate her for it.

"Tell me!" Arazan's voice cracked like a whip, and the demon nuzzled the stone floor, unwilling to raise his eyes to her.

"You are . . . my master," he said finally, in a small voice far removed from the furious roar he had used prior.

"Tell me you will obey me!" Arazan's voice was dominant now, and Maddie could hear the triumphant note in it as the sorceress realized all her work was coming to fruition.

There was the slightest hesitation, then Krakotomal whispered, "I will obey you." The words seemed to be wrung out of him as if he were on a rack.

"Again!"

"I will . . . obey you."

"Louder! You will obey me!"

"I will obey you!"

"Now come closer to my circle," Arazan commanded. The demon began slithering and scraping toward the pentacle, using the knuckles of his scaly wings for support and pushing his way with his powerful, clawed hind legs. His head was down, his eyes fixed on the floor.

Maddie, who had kept her eyes pinned on the demon so far, switched her gaze to Arazan. She was alarmed by the unholy expression of triumph on the woman's face. The sorceress had eyes only for the slithering, prostrate monster before her as she realized that her summoning spell had been successful, and the demon was now in her total control.

"That's close enough. Stop there," she commanded, when Krakotomal was two meters from the unbroken chalk line.

The demon stopped and began to sway back and forth, moaning in anguish and rage. Maddie realized he was studying the chalk line. He might be under Arazan's control, but the slightest fault in the pentacle would see him reassert his power and individuality.

Arazan realized what Krakotomal was doing and she laughed at him. "Look all you like, demon, but you won't find a break in the line. I checked it thoroughly."

Krakotomal's only reply was a grunt of frustration as his head continued to swing from side to side, searching for some imperfection, some fault, some gap in the chalk. But there was none.

Maddie slowly reached for her sling and loaded a shot into the pouch. She sensed the time was approaching when she would be called upon to break this impasse.

"Maddie! Now!"

Will's voice boomed across the cavern, and Maddie stepped clear of the rocks, left foot forward, right arm back, with the sling dangling down, ready to throw.

"Who was that!?" Arazan shrieked. Krakotomal rose onto his hind legs. Both of them peered toward the rocks where Will was concealed, where his voice had come from. It was Maddie's chance.

"Who's there?" screamed Arazan in a rage.

Krakotomal bellowed a challenge, sensing something had gone wrong with the sorceress's plan.

Maddie stepped forward into the cast, bringing the sling up and over, releasing at exactly the right moment, her eyes fixed on the target—the flat stone behind the small jar of water.

There was a whizzing sound as the shot flew across the cavern, followed almost instantly by the cracking sound it made as it slammed into the flat rock. The two sounds drew the attention of the demon and the sorceress, and they swung to look at the rock pile at the foot of the wall.

Then, disaster!

The shot was perfectly aimed, but the flat stone, unfortunately, wasn't perfectly flat. Slightly offset from the center, another stone, older and harder, was embedded in its surface, forming an almost imperceptible bump. It was this that the lead shot struck, causing it to ricochet back toward Maddie, but at the wrong angle, so that it missed the water jar by just over a centimeter, leaving it undisturbed as the lead projectile clattered across the stone floor of the cavern, bouncing and spinning.

"Who's there?" screamed Arazan once more, and again, Krakotomal unleashed a bellow of fury.

Maddie froze. Her cloak was shielding her from their sight,

and the herbs around her neck were confusing Arazan's senses. But both the demon and the witch knew there was someone, or something, in the cavern with them. Arazan was the first to recover her senses. She swung back to study the rock face where Will was concealed—from where she had heard the first shouted order to Maddie.

Arazan leaned forward, her eyes slitted against the gloom and the shadows, and the traces of green smoke still drifting through the cavern. She thought she could see . . . something . . . halfway up the rock wall. Krakotomal followed her gaze. His sight was keener and he penetrated the camouflage colors of Will's cloak, vaguely sighting a form among the rocks but not sure what it was.

Maddie thought fast. Any chance of using the sling was gone. The flat rock was knocked hopelessly out of position by the impact of the first shot. There was only one chance to complete her mission and she had to do it quickly, or Will would be exposed to the demon and to Arazan.

She dropped the sling and scrabbled for her bow, which was leaning against the rocks close to hand. As she seized it, her other hand whipped an arrow out of her quiver with the skill of long practice. She nocked it smoothly and brought the bow up, drawing back the arrow until the fletching touched the corner of her mouth.

She was an expert shot with the sling, but for fine accuracy like this, the bow was a better choice. She resisted the temptation to hold the shot, trying to make sure of her aim. That wasn't the way she had been trained to shoot. She was trained to draw, aim and shoot almost in one movement. Taking extra time over the action would only result in a lack of accuracy.

And now she released, with her aiming point just below the clay jar full of water.

The arrow hit the small pile of stones supporting the jar and slid in underneath it, with a screeching sound of metal on rock. The jar was untouched but the stones were scattered, spraying out from under the jar so that it tilted *forward*, falling down toward the pentacle, shattering on the rocks below and spilling its contents onto the slope leading toward the chalk line. The water gushed eagerly toward the pentacle, hitting the powdered chalk and washing it away.

It was only a small gap—less than two centimeters. But Krakotomal, his eyes drawn toward the spot by the sound of the arrow hitting the rocks, saw it immediately and bounded across the cavern.

Arazan saw it a few seconds after him and realized, with horror, that her protective barrier was breached.

"No-o-o-o-o-o!" she screamed as she started toward the tiny gap in the chalk line. But she was too late.

Krakotomal reached the hole, and Maddie watched in horrified fascination as his huge body seemed to shrink down, flowing like smoke through the gap, then re-formed on the far side—inside the pentacle with the sorceress.

He rose onto his powerful hind legs, beat his wings in the air and roared in triumph.

34

ARAZAN SCREAMED IN TERROR. SHE COWERED BACK, BUT THERE was nowhere for her to go. Krakotomal was upon her in one sudden leap, folding his scaly wings around her and tearing at her with the cruel claws on his powerful hind legs.

She beat at him with her fists but to no effect. Her physical strength was nothing compared with his power. Maddie saw the sorceress's robe shredding under his assault. Blood was flowing from several deep wounds in her legs, and the cavern echoed to the roaring of the demon and Arazan's futile, terrified screams.

In vain, she tried to command him, in a weak, trembling voice. "Release me! Release me! You must obey me!" she screamed.

But the demon threw back his head and bellowed with laughter. "You cannot command me now! The pentacle is broken and I am in control!"

Maddie stood transfixed, watching the horrific scene play out. She had no sympathy for Arazan—the woman had proved herself to be thoroughly evil. But nobody, she thought, deserved such a horrific fate.

Then she saw movement in the rocks on the far wall, and

Will emerged from his hiding place, bounding down the piled rocks, his hands clutching something before him.

Arazan saw him too and screamed an appeal to him. "Help me! Please! Help me!"

Krakotomal had his back to Will, but now he realized that Arazan was appealing to someone and he turned his head to see the Ranger kneeling by the gap in the chalk line. Too late, he realized what was about to happen.

"No-o-o-o!" he roared. The word was drawn out and echoed around the rock walls of the cavern. Krakotomal released Arazan and the sorceress fell to the rock floor, bleeding and groaning in agony. Then he gathered himself, ready to leap across the pentacle to the break in the line.

But before he could move, Will opened his hands and dumped a pile of chalk dust onto the gap in the pentacle, sealing it once more.

Krakotomal flew across the intervening space, a fraction of a second too late. Just before he reached Will, something stopped him in midair—an invisible barrier that rose up from the pentacle's chalked outline. Krakotomal hung in midair for a second, then rebounded, falling with a clash of scaly wings to the hard stone floor inside the pentacle.

Maddie heaved a sigh of relief. She and Will had believed that if the pentacle was restored, Krakotomal would be unable to cross it again. But they hadn't been sure. Now they knew. He was trapped inside the pentacle. And Arazan was there with him, badly injured and unable to escape.

He snarled and lunged at the invisible barrier, trying to reach Will, to drag him inside. But the barrier held.

A few meters away, Arazan huddled on the rock floor, torn and bleeding, whimpering with fear as she realized that the demon now had control over her rather than vice versa. But for the moment, Krakotomal had lost interest in her. He snarled and roared abuse and hatred at the gray-cloaked figure only a few meters away from him.

A few meters, perhaps, but secure against the demon's attempts to breach the pentacle.

Time and again, Krakotomal hurled his powerful body against the unseen barrier. And time and again, he was repulsed. The terrible sound of his fury filled the room.

Then, realizing his attempts to escape from the pentacle were doomed to failure, he grew quiet. He rose onto his rear legs, wings folded back behind him. A cunning light filled those triangular eyes. When he spoke again, his voice was soft-toned and wheedling.

"Tell me, mortal, what do you want? I can give you riches. I can give you power. I can give you anything your heart desires. Just set me free from this prison, and I will grant you any wish."

Arazan rose weakly to her hands and knees, gesturing desperately for Will to hear her.

"No!" she cried, her voice weak and quavering. "Don't listen to him!"

Krakotomal swung back toward her, his face a mask of fury as he dropped the pretense of friendliness.

"Be silent!" he snarled. Then he turned back to Will and resumed his cajoling tone. "She's evil. She cannot be trusted. Tell me what you want most in the world, and I will grant it to you."

The demon was unused to dealing with mortals. He seemed

to be unaware that his furious bellowing at Arazan was seriously at odds with his attempt to influence Will and served only to undermine his credibility.

"I want you to return to wherever you came from," Will said evenly.

Krakotomal laughed. Unlike his earlier triumphant bellowing, this was a warm sound—friendly, understanding. "No, no, no," he said. "It's too late for that. I am here now, and here I will stay. Now tell me what you want most in the world, and I will grant it to you. You have my word."

The soft, honeyed tones were totally at odds with the horrific appearance of the demon. Yet there was a mesmeric quality to the voice and the words, and Maddie found herself leaning forward, nodding her head as she mentally urged Will to consider the demon's offer. Abruptly, she shook herself and dispelled the feeling. Will said nothing in response, but he reached inside his jerkin and produced a single sheet of parchment. He unfolded it and began to read aloud.

"*Atimal shiban jakuru. Jakuru nutre shiban. Atimal Krakotomal beast.*"

For a moment, the demon recoiled a half pace, and his eyes glowed red with fury once more. Then he quickly masked his anger and laughed. "A banishment spell? Who has taught you this?"

Maddie realized that Will was holding the banishment spell Eveningstar had given him. Yet it seemed to be having no effect.

"You fool," said Krakotomal. "The spell of banishment is worthless on its own. It needs to be accompanied by the moon—"

He broke off quickly, suddenly aware that he was giving Will more information than he wanted the Ranger to have. But

Maddie realized what he had been about to say and her hand dropped to the feathered ends of the arrows in her quiver.

"The silver, Will!" she called to him. "The spell needs to be accompanied by silver!"

She withdrew an arrow from her quiver, checking quickly to make sure it was one with a silver warhead. Will looked quickly across at her and nodded, then he began to read the spell once more.

"*Atimal shiban jakuru. Jakuru nutre shiban. Atimal Krakotomal beast.*"

Maddie nocked the arrow to her string and drew back. Krakotomal, his eyes drawn to her when she had called out, snarled a challenge at her, spreading his wings wide and rearing up on his hind legs—which only served to make him an easier target.

Maddie released and the arrow flashed across the cavern.

And stopped in midair.

Incredibly, as it reached the invisible barrier surrounding the pentacle, something seemed to seize hold of the arrow, dragging it to a full stop so that it hung in midair.

Then, slowly, it began to move again, sliding forward as it penetrated the invisible shield.

"*Atimal shiban jakuru. Jakuru nutre shiban. Atimal Krakotomal beast,*" Will chanted. Then, suddenly, the arrow was through the barrier and in an instant it resumed its original flashing speed. It covered the few meters to Krakotomal in a heartbeat and struck the demon high on his body, punching through the scales that protected him and burying the silver warhead deep in his flesh.

Krakotomal screamed as the arrow hit home. He staggered back away from Will, striking at the arrow with his left wing.

This served only to break off the arrow shaft, leaving the silver warhead buried deep in his flesh.

"*Atimal shiban jakuru. Jakuru nutre shiban. Atimal Krakotomal beast.*"

Will continued the chant as Maddie realized that Krakotomal's shape was becoming fainter while green smoke began to swirl around him. The hard lines of his body were softening, and as he realized this was happening, he screamed out in defiance.

Then, with a last, desperate lunge, he leapt at Arazan's cowering form, wrapping his massive wings around her, hugging her to him in a desperate, deadly embrace.

"No-o-o-o!" she screamed as she realized what was about to happen.

But the green mist swirled up, and she too became less defined, seeming to fade and dissolve into the swirling smoke until she blended with the massive shape of the demon, and together, they spiraled down into nothing.

And then both were gone, leaving only a swirl of green smoke and the smell of burned sulfur behind them.

35

WILL STUMBLED AND SANK DOWN ONTO ONE OF THE LARGER boulders, totally exhausted by the strain of the preceding few minutes. His shoulders drooped and his head sagged wearily. He wiped the back of his hand across his forehead.

Alarmed, Maddie dashed from her hiding place and ran to him. She dropped to her knees beside him, her arms around his shoulders.

"Are you hurt?" she asked anxiously. "Are you all right?"

Will looked up at her and shook his head, giving her a weary smile. "I'm fine," he assured her. "Just very, very tired."

She hugged him to her, feeling relief flooding through her as she realized he was uninjured. "I'm not surprised," she said. She leaned back from him and turned her head to study the pentacle. Along with the remaining traces of green sulfurous smoke, there was another scorch mark on the stone floor, on the spot where Arazan and Krakotomal had crossed back into another world.

"My god, that was dreadful!" she said. "I have never ever seen anything like that."

"And I don't want to ever see anything like it again," Will

said, shaking his head as he remembered the terror of the preceding ten minutes. "At least," he added ruefully, "we were right about the pentacle keeping Krakotomal confined once I repaired the breach."

She shuddered at the memory of the demon hurling himself against the invisible barrier. "We took a heck of a chance on that," she said. "At least, you did."

"It seemed logical," Will said.

She shook her head. "Maybe so. But next time, I'd want to know for sure, not just assume that *it seems logical.*"

"Next time?" Will said. "Are you planning on a next time?"

Maddie grimaced at the thought. "Not in a million years," she said in a heartfelt tone. "Once is enough for me. In fact, it's more than enough." She gestured at the pentacle. "What do we do with this? Do we leave it?"

Will shook his head. "We destroy it. I don't want someone else deciding they might use it to resummon Krakotomal—or to bring back Arazan, for that matter."

He rose wearily from his seat on the boulder and walked to the chalk line marking the pentacle. He began to scuff the chalk with the sole of his boot, scattering it and obliterating the five-pointed star and the circle that surrounded it. Maddie joined him, and in a few minutes, there was nothing left of the pentacle other than an irregular smear of chalk dust on the cavern floor. Will stood back to survey the result of their efforts.

"That should do it," he said.

Maddie eyed him curiously. "Who else did you think might use it?"

He shrugged. "Nobody in particular. I just feel better knowing that it's gone."

"So, what's our next step?" Maddie asked.

He paused for a few seconds. To tell the truth, he hadn't thought much beyond stopping Arazan and banishing Krakotomal back to where he had come from. Now he realized there were several loose ends that needed tying up.

"We still have to get rid of that last direwolf," he said. "It's too dangerous to leave roaming around."

She nodded. Funny, she thought. The direwolves had been the reason they had traveled to Celtica in the first place. But the discovery of Arazan's horrifying activities had relegated them to a secondary problem.

"What about the Wargals?" she asked.

He shook his head. "They shouldn't be a problem. As I recall, once Morgarath died, the mind lock between him and his Wargals was broken and they reverted to their natural behavior. Left to their own devices, they're basically harmless, peaceful creatures. I imagine the same will hold true of Arazan's tribe. With her gone, they shouldn't be a problem."

"That's a relief. I can't say I—"

Maddie was interrupted by a sound from the entrance to the tunnel. A low-pitched, terrifying, growling noise.

They both spun to face the entrance. A dark figure crouched there, lit from behind by the flickering torches that illuminated the tunnel.

Marko, the leader of Arazan's Wargals, was facing them, his fangs bared, the heavy iron spear that was the favored weapon of the Wargals clutched in the ready position before him.

"You killed Mis'ress," he snarled, in his slurred voice.

As they had noted before, Marko was an anomaly among the Wargals. His intelligence was more highly developed, and he had even managed to speak in simple sentences, although the words themselves were distorted by the nonhuman shape of his mouth and jaws.

Apparently, that higher level of intelligence provided him with the ability to retain his awareness and enmity without the overriding influence of Arazan's control.

He advanced into the cavern, his eyes fixed on Will, moving slowly and menacingly toward the two Rangers.

Maddie looked round for her bow. But she had left it among the rocks when she rushed out to Will. Automatically, she felt for her sling, then realized it was on the ground where she had dropped it after her ill-fated shot at the flat rock behind the water jar. Will's bow was among the rocks where he had left it when he had rushed down to repair the pentacle chalk line.

Will stepped between her and the advancing Wargal chief. His hand dropped to the hilt of his saxe, and it slid from its scabbard with a metallic *shrriing*.

Marko stopped at the sound. His eyes narrowed as he saw the glittering steel blade in Will's hand. Then he assessed the threat and realized that it wasn't a sword, but merely an oversized knife. His confidence returned, and he lunged forward at Will, jabbing out with the short, heavy spear.

The jarring, scraping sound of metal on metal rang through the cavern as Will's saxe intercepted the spear. He didn't try to block the spear thrust directly—the saxe wasn't heavy enough to do that, and even the two-knife defense wouldn't be strong enough against the heavy iron weapon. Rather, he deflected it, flicking it off to one side so that Marko stumbled forward as the spear cut through empty air, encountering no real opposition.

Furious, the Wargal swung his spear in a roundhouse blow

aimed at Will's head. The Ranger ducked easily underneath it and slashed the razor-sharp edge of his saxe across Marko's exposed left arm.

Belatedly, Maddie drew her own saxe and started forward. But Will's voice stopped her.

"Stay out of it, Maddie," he ordered.

She stepped back, realizing that any action on her part would only serve to distract Will, who seemed to have the situation well under control.

Which was, in fact, the case. Marko was strong and fast. And he was imbued with the single-minded savagery that made Wargals such dangerous opponents. But he wasn't a highly trained fighter. Morgarath had drilled his Wargals for years, teaching them weapon skills and fighting tactics. But Morgarath had been a warrior himself, and a highly capable one. Arazan wasn't. She had utilized the Wargals' natural strength and commitment to do her bidding but had done nothing to teach them how to handle their weapons. Most of the time, when they were facing miners and farmers, this had been more than enough.

As a result, Marko was a clumsy and unimaginative fighter, relying on brute force and power to overcome an opponent.

Except now he was faced with an opponent who was not only far more skillful than he was, but highly experienced as well.

He feinted forward with the spear. Will read the feint and didn't react. The saxe remained thrust out in front of him, razor-sharp and deadly, barring Marko's way. Marko feinted again, hoping to drive Will back. Once more, Will read the feint and didn't react.

Now rage took hold of Marko. With an inarticulate cry, he

made a full-blooded lunge at the Ranger, driving the spear out to its fullest reach, throwing himself off-balance. Will sidestepped the lunge and the spear slid past him as Marko stumbled in its wake.

And as he did, Will brought the saxe up with a lightning-fast but fully controlled lunge at Marko's upper body. The blade struck Marko's leather jerkin, sliding into the gap between two of the protective metal plates sewn onto it. It bit into the hard leather, the razor-sharp, super-hardened blade penetrating easily through the leather and then the flesh behind it.

Marko felt a savage flare of agony as the saxe went home, and for a moment, he and Will stood chest to chest. He tried to comprehend what had just happened to him but couldn't find an answer.

Marko's fingers opened and the heavy iron spear fell, ringing, to the stone floor of the cavern. He tried to speak, but no words would come, only a massive grunt of pain. Will's face was half a meter away from his, but as he watched, it was becoming indistinct, seeming to fade from his vision. Then, as the Ranger backed away from him, everything went black as Marko continued to wonder what had just happened to him.

But there was no answer, just . . . nothing.

36

WILL STEPPED BACK FROM THE WARGAL'S INERT FORM WHERE it sprawled on the cavern floor. He shook his head sadly. Killing always saddened him, even when it involved a creature as brutal as Marko.

"He didn't need to do that," he said quietly. "It's something else to lay at Arazan's door." He turned to Maddie, who was watching silently. "Let's get out of here," he said.

They collected their bows and Maddie's sling and headed for the entrance to the passageway. At the doorway, Maddie turned and surveyed the cavern one last time. The smell of sulfur still hung in the air, but otherwise there was no sign of what had gone on here. Will nudged her with his elbow.

"Let's go," he said. "Keep an arrow nocked, just in case I'm wrong about the rest of the Wargals."

Silently, they retraced their path down the narrow passageway. The torches set along the walls were almost burned out by now. As they made their way out, two of the torches went out with a soft popping noise. The fact that the torches hadn't been renewed indicated that with Arazan's death, discipline and the normal routine among the Wargals had collapsed.

They paused at the exit from the cave complex, studying the outside area. There was no sign of any of the Wargals. None were on watch. Motioning for Maddie to follow him, Will ghosted across the open space to the rocks where they had been hiding during the day.

There was no outcry; no alarm sounded. There was no indication that anyone or anything had seen them. They noticed one or two of the Wargals curled up on the ground outside their hovels, deep in sleep.

There was no sign of the remaining direwolf. Will frowned as he leaned closer to Maddie, saying in a low voice: "It's too dark to see anything yet. Get some sleep and we'll hunt around in the morning."

Maddie leaned back against a rock, pulling her cloak tightly around her and huddling down in its warmth. "After what we've been through, I doubt I'll be able to sleep," she said.

Will smiled and patted her shoulder. "I'll wake you an hour before dawn," he said.

In spite of her protestations to the contrary, Maddie realized that she was exhausted. The tension and mental strain of the night were the equivalent of hours of hard physical labor. Her eyelids grew heavy. The cloak was warm and comforting, and within a few minutes she was breathing deeply, fast asleep.

Will woke her an hour before first light and settled down to get some rest himself. When dawn came, there was no sign of movement from the Wargals, so she let him sleep on. The sun was well above the eastern horizon when she heard movement from the Wargal camp.

She watched from her hiding place among the rocks as the

strange creatures began to stir. But there was a noticeable change in the way they behaved. Whereas before they had prowled anxiously around their campsite, looking warily for Marko and responding instantly to his orders, now they sat calmly among the rocks, or moved on all fours, searching for edible plants. They seemed more relaxed and less threatening. Also, she noticed, they had discarded their armor, and their weapons remained stacked where they had left them the night before.

She laid a light hand on Will's shoulder, and he was instantly awake, his eyes asking a question, alert for trouble. She reassured him with a wave of her hand and pointed to the Wargals.

"Seems you were right," she said quietly.

He rose to one knee and observed them for a few minutes. "Yes," he said at length. "They've reverted to their natural character. Any sign of the direwolf?"

She shook her head. "Not so far. I think it might have gone."

Will chewed his lip thoughtfully. "We'll have a quick bite to eat, then we'll scout around to see if we can pick up its tracks," he said. "I'm not happy about leaving that creature behind. It's caused enough trouble."

"Can we have a fire?" Maddie asked.

Will looked again at the Wargals. Four of them were awake now, shuffling and snuffling their way around the campsite. They appeared to be totally unthreatening.

"Yes. Let's," he said. "I've been too long without a cup of coffee inside me. Just keep well away from them while you're gathering the firewood."

His warning turned out to be unnecessary. As Maddie moved around the cleared area collecting twigs and light branches, the

Wargals, after an initial curious glance, seemed to pay her no attention at all.

They lit a small fire and boiled water from their canteens, luxuriating in the rich taste of the hot coffee while they toasted pieces of flatbread over the glowing coals.

"Oh, that's better," Will said as he drained his second cup. He rose, stretched and kicked sand over the fire to extinguish it. "Now let's see if we can find some sign of that wolf."

They cast around, heading inland initially, moving several meters apart with their eyes down on the ground searching for tracks.

"Don't become too fixated on the ground," Will cautioned her. "You don't want to look up to see you're on top of the ugly brute."

Maddie saw the good sense of his instruction. She realized, with a pang of guilt, that she had been concentrating totally on the rough sand and pebbles in front of her, searching for some sign that the direwolf had been that way. She began to consciously look up every few meters, checking the land ahead of her for sight of the huge wolf.

They moved in a wide semicircle without finding any trace of the beast. Eventually, they were back at their starting point, and Will gestured toward the track leading to the top of the plateau and the narrow path down the cliff to the Fissure.

"It may be heading back toward Celtica," he said, and they headed off in that direction.

It was easier to search here, as the open ground fell away and the track became narrower, funneled between the rocks and boulders that covered the ground. After several minutes, Maddie stopped and held her hand up.

"Here," she called softly.

Will moved over to stand beside her. Clearly defined in the loose pebbles and sand that formed the base of the track was the imprint of a large canine paw. A meter or so farther beyond it was a second, then a third another few meters along.

"Yes. That's him all right. And he's heading back toward the Fissure. I'll look for tracks. You keep watch that he doesn't double back on us. And keep an arrow ready on your string."

Maddie licked her lips. They were dry with the realization that the direwolf was somewhere ahead of them, somewhere among the scattered boulders and rocks that covered the terrain in that part of the plateau. She selected an arrow from her quiver and set it on the string, holding it in place with the forefinger of her left hand curled around the bow stave. Then she moved off again, staying several meters behind Will, who was intent on searching for more tracks in the gravelly sand. He gave a low cry as he spotted more indentations. Maddie kept her eyes swiveling, looking from side to side, up into the boulders, then along the track ahead of them, searching for a sign of the direwolf's shaggy fur among the rocks.

"Don't forget to look behind us," Will reminded her.

She grunted in reply, realizing that she had been neglecting to look in that direction. From then on, she turned to face their rear every three or four paces, taking several steps backward as she checked that all was clear.

But there was no sign of the wolf.

Eventually, they reached the rim of the plateau. They paused at the top of the steep, narrow trail that led down to the bridge far below them. Will called a halt and Maddie relaxed. She realized that her shoulders had been tensed for the last several kilometers as she guarded against a possible surprise attack from the huge wolf. The uncertainty, the knowledge that at any moment it could appear, charging out of the rocks, leaping at them, had kept her nerves at breaking point.

Will studied the ground around the top of the track for several meters in each direction, making sure that the direwolf hadn't doubled back to take up a position behind them. But the pad marks continued steadily down the trail, with no sign that the beast had returned.

"It's kept going," he declared after several minutes. "Unless it's learned to walk backward in its own tracks."

"So it's heading back to Celtica?" Maddie asked.

Will nodded several times. "It looks that way," he said. "Mind you, it only makes sense. It knows there's good hunting in Celtica and plenty of easy prey."

"And with Arazan gone, there's nothing to keep it up here on the plateau," Maddie said.

"That's true." Will took one last look around the desolate plateau and the gray tumble of rocks and boulders that surrounded them. He realized that he'd be glad to be rid of the place. Very glad.

"Let's get after it," he said, jerking his thumb toward the cliff track. "Before it has time to get lost somewhere in Celtica."

And, nocking an arrow to his bowstring, he headed down the steep, narrow path that led back to the bridge across the Fissure.

37

THEY MADE THEIR WAY DOWN THE STEEP, WINDING TRACK. IT was narrow underfoot, and there was a yawning drop to the left side. Maddie peered over the edge once, seeing the ruins of the burned bridge and the flimsy footbridge they had crossed far below them. And beyond them, the dizzying depths of the Fissure plunged away to the unseen bottom, hidden in shadow. For a moment, peering down into the Fissure, she felt her head swimming as vertigo threatened to claim her. She moved back from the drop, pressing against the hard rock wall until her head cleared.

Will noticed her action. "Don't look down," he cautioned her belatedly.

She shook herself. "I won't do it again," she said. As they continued down the track, she kept her right shoulder pressed lightly against the wall, staying as far away from the edge as she could manage.

Will, who had a more reliable head for heights, seemed untroubled by the immense drop only a meter or so away. He moved swiftly down the trail, his eyes searching for signs that the direwolf had preceded them.

Although the track was mostly formed from solid rock, there were sufficient patches of coarse sand and fine gravel where he could see that the direwolf had gone before them. As they came to each bend in the track, he slowed down, readying his bow in case they should stumble unexpectedly on the direwolf. But each time, the tension flowed out of him in an anticlimax as he rounded the bend and saw the way ahead was clear.

Moving carefully that way and keeping an eye for signs of the direwolf's passing, they reached the bottom, stepping out onto the wide ledge where the bridges had been built.

"It's been here," Will said, indicating more tracks in the coarse sand, leading to the rope footbridge that spanned the terrifying drop that was the Fissure.

He paused before setting foot on it. The flimsy structure was swaying gently in the ever-present wind. But he knew that movement would be accentuated once he started to cross. He frowned. Crossing the bridge, he'd need at least one hand for the rope handrail. And that meant he would be unable to hold his bow ready.

He gestured to Maddie to move to the side, so she had a clear view of the bridge and the far side of the Fissure.

"Stay here," he told her, "and keep an eye out for the wolf. I don't want it jumping me when I'm halfway across."

Maddie nodded wordlessly. She licked her lips, which had gone dry again with the uncertainty of their journey down the steep, winding track, never knowing if each twist and turn might find them facing the direwolf. She already had an arrow nocked. Now she set herself in a side-on stance to the bridge, with her left foot advanced and the string slightly drawn. She could see the first five or six meters of clear ground on the other side.

After that, the jumbled rocks and boulders obscured her sight, providing plenty of potential cover for the direwolf. If it did appear, she'd have only seconds to react and to shoot. She'd seen how quickly the massive beasts could cover ground.

"Ready," she said quietly, the arrow pointing down at the ground a few meters in front of her. Will nodded, replaced his arrow in his quiver and stepped onto the bridge, flexing his knees to cope with the sudden jerky movement as it took his weight. Holding the bow ready in his left hand, he placed his right on the rope side rail and began to make his way across. The farther he moved from the edge of the drop, the more the bridge bounced and swayed under his feet. He crouched slightly to retain his balance and slid his feet along the rough planks, testing the strength and solidity of each foothold before committing his full weight to it and moving warily forward. He shifted his weight carefully from one foot to the other, always conscious of the danger of a rotten plank or a frayed section of rope.

As he reached the midpoint, the bridge's motion became more severe. It seemed to develop a life of its own, its movements devoid of any rhythm. It flexed up and down and swayed side to side under his weight. The two distinct movements created a swaying, plunging motion that was almost impossible to predict.

He wondered how the clumsy, graceless Wargals had managed the bridge, then he shrugged. Maybe their having no imagination worked in their favor, he thought. They may have had no idea of how dangerous the crossing was.

As he drew closer to the far edge and the bridge angled upward more steeply, he shortened his stride. Then he heaved a sigh of relief as he stepped clear of the bridge and onto the firm footing of the far bank.

He paused, letting his pulse settle, then took an arrow from his quiver and nocked it to the bowstring. He scanned the rocks ahead of him. There was no sign of the direwolf, although he could clearly see its tracks leading away from the bridge where he stood and disappearing into the mass of rocks and boulders that fringed the track leading back to Celtica.

Once he was sure the direwolf wasn't in the near vicinity, he turned and signaled to Maddie to make her way across.

Bow ready, he moved a few meters away from the bridge, his eyes constantly scanning the ground ahead. He heard the low creaking sound of the bridge's support ropes as Maddie began to make her careful way across to join him. But he resisted the temptation to watch her, keeping his gaze on the track and the broken ground that could be concealing the direwolf if it doubled back on the enemies tracking it.

After several minutes, he heard the crunch of her footsteps in the gravel behind him as she stepped off the bridge.

"I'm glad that's over," she said. She moved up beside him and nocked an arrow to her own bow, scanning left and right ahead of them, ready for any sign of the huge wolf.

But there was none.

"Let's get the horses and get out of here," said Will.

Tug and Bumper reacted happily to the sight of their owners. Tug rattled his mane, shaking his head rapidly from side to side. Bumper treated Maddie to one of his trademark headbutts as she fondled his soft muzzle. The piles of grain that Will had left for them were gone, so he opened the feed sack and poured more onto the ground. The two horses munched happily, then moved to the small rock pool and drank.

They saddled the horses, but when Maddie went to mount, Will held out a hand to stop her.

"We'll go on foot," he said. "The horses can follow behind." Then, in answer to Maddie's questioning gaze, he elaborated. "If we run into the wolf, we'll have to shoot fast. Our bows are too long if we're mounted."

She nodded her understanding, and he gestured toward the narrow path through the rocks. "Let's go," he said. "Keep an eye behind us."

They set out on the track that would lead them back to Tenruath and Poddranyth. Will led the way, scanning the ground continually for signs that the direwolf had passed this way before them. There were plenty. The beast didn't seem to be worried about concealing its tracks. The big canine paw prints could be seen in every patch of soft ground as they followed the narrow trail through the rocks and broken landscape.

Maddie resumed her role as rear guard, turning to scan the trail behind them every five meters so, and walking backward for several paces as she did so. The horses followed meekly behind her, although both of them emitted warning rumbles from time to time.

"They can scent that it's been here," Will said.

Maddie nodded, calming the horses. The longer they went without sighting the direwolf, the more tense she became. Somehow, she sensed that the gigantic beast wouldn't be content to have them trailing it; sooner or later, it would turn back and ambush them.

She began to even half wish that it *would* attack them. Every bend in the track, every blind corner they rounded was a potential ambush site. Each time they pushed round a bend, bows raised and half-drawn in anticipation of a surprise attack, there was a huge letdown of tension as they found the path ahead empty.

The expectation and the rise and sudden release of tension was exhausting. Time after time, they prepared to confront the direwolf, only to find the track free of danger. The continual anticlimaxes sapped their reserves of energy and began to blunt their fine edge of preparedness.

"Maybe it's gone," she said, as for the twentieth time they prepared to confront the beast and found the path ahead of them empty of any threat.

Will shook his head. "It'll be here," he said. "Don't get complacent. Don't lose your edge. Keep your eyes open and be ready."

Guiltily, she realized that it had been several minutes since she had checked their back trail, and then only in the most cursory way. She turned back now and looked for any sign of danger. But the path behind them was clear. She was glad that Will was leading the way and that he would be the first to confront the creature. His massive bow was far more powerful than hers, and his years of experience meant he was a better, steadier shot than she was. She had confidence in her own ability and accuracy under pressure, but she had more confidence in his. He was Will Treaty, who so many people called the greatest of all Rangers, with the possible exception of Halt. He was fast, skillful, calm under pressure and seemingly indomitable. When she thought about it, she pitied any mere direwolf who might confront him.

So they continued, following the paw prints of the giant wolf, preparing for the worst at each twist or turn in the track, and confronting . . . nothing. The constant stopping and starting to prepare at each blind corner was costing them time. She glanced up at the sun and saw that it was dropping toward the mountains in the west. In another hour, it would be setting, and they would have to continue in the dark.

And the more the day wore on, the more she became convinced that they were on a wild-goose chase. The direwolf wasn't about to turn back and attack them. It had seen how they had coped with its siblings. If it was as cunning as she thought it to be, it would have shown them a clean pair of heels, bounding off down the track and out into the wilds of Celtica—the fields and rocks and mines where it could hide until they were long gone.

After all, there was easier prey for it to stalk among the miners and farmers of Celtica. They weren't armed with powerful longbows and barbed war arrows.

They came to another bend. Will stopped, motioned for her to do the same, and brought his bow up ready. Then, moving quickly, he darted round the corner in the track, bow coming up as he brought it to the half draw. He crouched, knees slightly bent and ready to counter a direwolf's deadly rush.

But there was nothing there. It was yet another false alarm, and Maddie let go a long sigh of relief, mixed with frustration. Like Will, she had half drawn her arrow. Now she let it down and stood upright, out of her ready shooter's crouch.

The track lay empty ahead of them, another blind corner only fifteen paces away. She gave a perfunctory glance behind them and followed Will toward the bend in the trail, convinced now that they were wasting their time.

As he paused and prepared to round the next blind corner, she wondered at his patience and commitment. Once again, he was prepared and tensed. She shook her head. It was a waste of energy and time. This bend in the track would be like the thirty or forty that had preceded it—a false alarm, a sudden flood of adrenaline followed by an almost instant letdown.

Halfheartedly, she moved up behind Will, quickly checked the trail behind them, took up the tension on her bow and lunged around the bend in the trail behind him, bow coming up and ready.

38

YET AGAIN, NOTHING.

No sign of the wolf. No sudden rush of claws across the rocky ground. No massive, yawning fangs. Just the empty track once more and the sickening surge of relief in the pit of her stomach.

She relaxed, easing the tension on her bow, and let Will begin to pace slowly down the next section of clear track before them. The next corner was twenty meters away, and then they would have to go through the whole process once more.

And once more, she was now convinced, they would confront nothing.

The low, menacing growl seemed to come from all around them, and she felt the hairs on the back of her neck rising and her skin dimpling with fear. Will stopped, his bow coming up. Frantically, Maddie scanned the path ahead.

Then she saw it.

The direwolf was poised on top of a large rock several meters from the next twist in the track. It had finally turned back on the infuriating enemies who persisted in following it. Its eyes glowed yellow in the failing light, and it bared its fangs in a silent snarl.

Both horses sounded an instant alarm, but Maddie silenced them with a wave of her hand, her eyes fixed on the monster crouching ahead of them.

Will stepped in front of her, bringing his bow up.

"Stay back," he cautioned, and she stepped behind him, glad that his huge bow was between her and the terrifying beast that faced them. She watched over his shoulder as the direwolf crouched, gathering its hind legs under it, then propelled itself off the rock in a powerful leap, jaws wide open, huge fangs catching the light.

Smoothly, without seeming to hurry, Will brought his arrow back to full draw, the creature's chest filling his sighting picture. His fingers began to let the string slip away as he released . . .

With a loud *BANG!* the bowstring snapped.

The bow, suddenly unrestrained, snapped forward with a terrible jolt. In less than a second, it went from a smooth full curve to a wildly vibrating straight line, nearly tearing itself from Will's grasp.

The arrow, released from the tension of the bowstring, fell harmlessly away, clattering on the rocks. Then the wolf was upon him, driving him back with the force of the huge leap from the rocks, snarling and snapping in rage.

Will went down under its charge, jerking his face back to avoid those massive jaws. He had time to grip the bow stave in both hands and bring it up crosswise, thrusting it sideways into the slavering jaws of the monster, which bit down on the leather-wrapped grip.

Maddie sensed the two horses were about to charge to Will's rescue. She realized that if they did, they would probably block her shot.

"Stay!" she commanded, and they both froze, still whinnying in alarm but obeying her command.

Using the strength of both arms, Will pushed back against the wolf, forcing its head back away from him. Enraged, the wolf shook its massive head and released the bowstave. It pulled back, rearing up and raising its head to emit a shattering howl of rage.

And provided Maddie with a near-perfect target.

In one movement, she drew, sighted and shot. Her arrow flashed across the intervening space and went straight into the wolf's wide-open jaws, penetrating deep into its mouth, then reaching farther still, severing the spinal column where it reached the brain, killing the wolf instantly.

The enraged roar died away to a strangled grunt, and the massive beast slumped dead on top of Will. He struggled in vain under the deadweight of the huge wolf.

"Get me out of here," he said, and Maddie moved to help him.

Late in the afternoon, three days after they left Arazan's cave complex, they crossed the bridge and rode into Poddranyth, holding their horses to a gentle trot as they made their way down the main street and out the other end of the village. Word of their passing ran around the little settlement, and people emerged from their houses to watch them go.

They followed the road north, heading for Eveningstar's cottage. As they reached the track that spiraled up on the left to her house, Maddie noted that the mist that had previously obscured the path had dispersed.

They rode uphill and rounded the last bend to find the slightly built woman waiting for them outside her cottage, a smile of welcome on her face.

"Good to see you again," she said as they dismounted. Then she moved forward quickly to embrace them both.

"Arazan is gone," Will told her, "and the demon with her."

"I know," she said calmly. "I was watching when you confronted them." She gave Will an admiring look. "You did very well for someone not skilled in the black arts."

She led the way inside and motioned them to seats at the table by the crackling fire in the grate.

"I'll make tea," she said. "It's a cold afternoon to be riding."

Will reached into his satchel and produced a small sack containing the last of their supply of coffee. "Coffee would be better," he said.

She smiled. "Of course it would." She busied herself making a pot, poured them both large mugs and placed a bowl of honey on the table in front of them.

"I lost sight of you when you came back down the cliffs to the footbridge," she said. "I take it you took care of the direwolves as well as Arazan and her green friend?"

Will nodded. "Yes. The last one came back across the Fissure and tried to ambush us." He nodded to Maddie. "Maddie shot it. There'll be no more direwolves in Celtica."

"The people will be pleased to hear it," she said. She turned her gaze on Maddie now. "You shot it?"

Maddie nodded. She sensed that Will didn't want to go into detail over their encounter with the direwolf.

"I was in the better position," she said simply.

Eveningstar's gaze switched from one to the other. She sensed there was more that they could say about the direwolf's death. But she also sensed that they weren't about to elaborate. Will rose abruptly and went out to where their horses waited outside the door. He returned a few moments later with a large bundle over his arm. He placed it on the floor, where Eveningstar looked at it curiously.

"It's the direwolf's pelt," he said. "We thought you should have it."

Eveningstar knelt and ran her hand over the thick fur. She nodded several times.

"I'm honored," she said. Then she rose to her feet again and indicated the bedding by the fireplace.

"Will you stay the night again?" she invited.

But Will shook his head. "We'll get going. But thanks for the offer." He gestured to Maddie, and she drained her coffee cup and followed him to the door.

Eveningstar followed them. "Come and see me if you're ever in Celtica again," she said.

Will smiled. "I will. Although I'm sure you'll understand I'll be in no hurry to return."

He swung up into the saddle. Maddie was about to follow, but Eveningstar checked her. She reached forward and touched the sprig of rosemary still hanging around Maddie's neck.

"Still wearing this, I see?" she queried.

Maddie shrugged. "I'm used to it. Didn't realize it was still there."

Eveningstar nodded. "Rosemary," she said. "It's for remembrance."

Carefully, Maddie removed the cord from around her neck and laid the small bouquet of dried herbs on the window ledge.

"I'll leave it here," she said. "There's a lot about the past few days I'd rather forget."

READ ALL OF THE
BROTHERBAND BOOKS

READ ALL OF THE
RANGER'S APPRENTICE BOOKS

READ THE RANGER'S APPRENTICE: THE EARLY YEARS

READ THE RANGER'S APPRENTICE: THE ROYAL RANGER